THERE ARE ALIENS
AMONG US

COMMENTARY, VIEWS,
AND AN ORIGINAL NOVELLA BY BUD SELIGSON

Lost Age Publishing
2017

Printed in the United States of America

Cover art and interior design by: Cyrusfiction Productions.

First Edition Paperback
ISBN: 978-1-946480-02-6

9018 Balboa Boulevard
Suite #562
Northridge, CA 91325

TABLE OF CONTENTS

DEDICATION

With exception of doing the research and touring locations, the life of a writer tends to be very solitary and often boring. Never more so for me, as when I am working under a deadline. Every year, my wife Diane, puts up with the long hours, and the fact that, even when I am home, I am often mentally elsewhere. I am a lucky man to be married to such an awesome, and understanding woman.

—Bud Seligson

What we have here is a riddle, wrapped in a mystery,
inside of an enigma.

—Bud Seligson

FORMER GHOST WRITER TELLS IT ALL. (WELL ... ALMOST ALL)

by Bud Seligson

I guess it is O.K. To be sad, now that I am not writing as a ghost writer anymore.

It's very hard to walk away from something that I had a lot of fun doing for the past 50 years.

The story lines with Leonardo da Vinci, Otzi the bronze-age iceman, Nostradamus, Big Ed the cowboy, and this novel, have consumed me completely as I work on the plot lines and adventures.

These might be my very last thoughts on ghost-writing unless on our future comment page, some of you, my special readers, ask for some continued thoughts from me on ghosting or being a story-doctor for the Hollywood studios.

Anyway, here are some final ghost-writing thoughts. I hope you find them as much fun to read as I have had writing them.

What do Hillary Clinton, Madonna and president Obama have in common?

The answer is that they have all used ghost writers.

Celebrities, entrepreneurs, politicians and business leaders, routinely hire ghost-writers to capture their words for print.

It is estimated that 60 percent of nonfiction books have been ghosted.

There are whispers among my fellow ghosts, that a few best-selling novelists have had help writing their best sellers.

While the ghost-writing that I have created, is as varied as the different stories that were requested, there always remains one constant thread running through them.

And that is that I am completely confidential. I do not spill the beans or talk about my contracted work unless I am told that it is okay to do so.

And I don't just write for the high-profile types, but for those who have stories that snatch at your heartstrings, and make it hard to swallow.

I also have been known to write a pretty good and sexy love scene or two.

Like many in my field, I have ghosted how-to-do books, business books, diet manuals, cookbooks, autobiographies and even some speeches.

I have worked with stay at home moms, and headline news-makers.

Ghostwriting is far from boring, but it is not for someone with a large ego, because your name goes on absolutely nothing.

But instead of having your name out there, the money is really good.

"Civilians" (that is people who do not know the book publishing industry) look confused when I say that I am a ghost, but this career choice is now on the rise with young people just coming up and getting into the industry.

Ghosts get business through referrals and publishing contacts such as agents and publishers, and by asking around town for work.

Some of my fellow ghosts even go so far as advertising.

Most ghosts think of their job as being like any other profession. We provide a service for others.

While I would never cut, or color my own hair, because I know that I would screw it up quite badly, but technically I am physically able to do so with a scissors and comb in hand.

Instead of doing these kinds of things myself, I go to a professional.

Much as a hair stylist would never reveal to whom she's given natural blond highlights, ghosts rarely reveal whom they have written for.

A major requirement for successful ghosting is to have the ability to listen and then reflect the flair, style, phrases, unusual worlds, witticisms, and other elements that make the person you agreed to work for unique.

Authors rarely rave about their ghost writers, so why be one? Here are a few good reasons:

- To get an issue out through the use of the author's celebrity status.
- To have fun and meet a challenge and get paid well for doing so.
- To show publishers and agents what you can do.

Thanks for reading my thoughts. My very best regards.

—Bud Seligson

INTRODUCTION

by Bud Seligson

Philosophers have always been known for two things: knowing what they don't know, and for asking questions about it.

Since Socrates demurred that he was the wisest man in all of Greece, because he was apparently the only man who knew what he didn't know.

Philosophers have asked more questions than they have ever answered.

They have raised more problems than they have ever resolved and this rings true with our storyline that will follow later.

***

Please be at ease. I'm not about to pretend that the following story is completely true.

Names and dates are real, but a stretch of my imagination was used for many parts.

Any story with my name on it must stand or fall as entertainment and entertainment only.

Where doubts or gaps occurred in the mass of notes, clippings, photographs and recollections of words spoken, I have supplied my own conjectures.

Names, places and incidents have possibly been changed as it seemed needful by myself.

Throughout the following narrative and storyline, please find the techniques of science fiction writing only.

***

It is never easy to write in a universe that was written about and created by another author.

One must study their words in order to forge new episodes that have consistency with the original thoughts and ideas, and yet contribute fresh insights that the reader might enjoy.

I could go on about the reasons why I wrote this adventure the way I did, but at this point I'll forgo any further comments.

I just wish to point out that I do not see this story as an end point to the expansion of our human race to other worlds.

It is as that old, time song that I used to hum when I was just a kid back in Chicago many years ago, "it's only just begun."

***

Educated people never (well, hardly ever) argue that vampires, werewolves and other things that go bump in the night actually exist.

One can enjoy a fantasy story without actually believing in elves, dwarfs, dragons, unicorns, or other such creatures of institutionalized fantasy.

***

The basic scientific underpinning for this tale is as sound as careful research can make it.

I have taken liberties with agreed-upon scientific anon where I felt it necessary for the sake of the story.

I have endeavored to use the stuff of myth and legend as a means to explore.

With an exploding star and a shattered planet, we link astronomical events with death and birth on earth.

Intellectual reptiles give rise to the legend of devils that haunt the dark hours of every human culture.

Dinosaurs that somehow survived into prehistoric times, leads to our legends of dragons and so on.

These are the ingredients of science fiction. The science must be accurate, yet the author must be free to invent new possibilities—as long as no one can show that they are totally impossible in our real world.

The characters must be believable, no matter how fantastic their adventures.

They must feel love and bleed as you and I do. Otherwise we do not have a story to read, we simply end up with a thesis.

***

During the ice age, human beings were exposed to the colder temperatures of the time, often having to make their homes in caves.

There they found greater comfort and security than in the open.

We still live in caves called houses, again for comfort and security.

Virtually no one would willingly sleep on the ground under the stars if they have a clear choice of housing.

It is possible that we may someday seek to add further to our comfort and security by building our houses underground—in new, man-made caves.

It may not seem, at first thought, a palatable suggestion since we have so many evil associations with the underground in legend and religion.

They all tell us that the underground is the realm of evil spirits and of the dead. It is often thought of as the location of an afterlife of torment.

This may be because dead bodies are buried underground, and because we see and hear about volcanic eruptions that make the underground appear to be a hellish place of fire and noxious gases.

Yet there are advantages to underground life.

There is something to be said for thinking about whole cities of humankind generally moving downward or having the innermost mile of earth's crust honeycombed with passages and structures like a gigantic human anthill.

Weather would no longer be of much importance to us since it is primarily a phenomenon of the atmosphere.

Rain, snow, sleet and fog would not trouble the underground at all.

Even temperature variations are limited to the open surface, and would not exist underground.

Whether it was night or day, summer or winter, temperature in the underground would remain equable and nearly constant.

The vast amounts of energy now expended in warming the surface surrounding us when they are too cold, and cooling them down when they are too warm, could be saved.

The damage done by weather to man-made structures and human beings, would be gone.

Transportation over local distances would be greatly simplified, but earthquakes would remain a great danger of course.

And also, very important, local time would no longer be important.

On the surface, the tyranny of day and night can't be avoided, and when it is morning in one place, it is noon in another, and evening somewhere else.

We could easily adjust our days to suit humanities convenience at all-times.

Does this sound interesting? It does to me and I hope to hear about it happening all around us in the very near future.

GALAXIES AND STARS
FORMATION OF ALL MATTER AND US

THE UNIVERSE'S BIG BANG.

Once at the beginning of our universe, approximately 13 billion years ago, there existed a super unimaginable hot explosion everywhere that is referred to as the Big Bang.

The temperature was 1,000 billion degrees, and most cosmologist generally agree that all forms of energy, matter, space and time were formed in that super-heated moment.

As space and time expanded, the matter (which included particles of photons and quarks, followed by full protons and neutrons) precipitated outward and away from that spot and location.

This precipitation or condensation took less than a second and during that second, particles and atoms traveled outward at the speed of light and are still on the move today.

A terrifically powerful energetic nucleus of atoms separated from each other and the result was the cooling universe that we have today.

It is still expanding outward with no end in sight (as far as we can tell).

***

On earth, things move in specific cycles.
That is why, after 4.6 billion years of existence, our wonderful planet is still young, active and full of life.

Water runs from the uplands in a downward movement to the sea. It moves quickly as rivers and seeping up as ground water.

It may be delayed for a while and collect in ponds and lakes, but it always lands in the ocean or occasionally in an inland sea.

It is the natural downward flow under the strong pull of gravity of which nothing can resist.

Why does all the water not end up in the seas, lakes and oceans which would have then left the land desert dry billions of years ago.

The answer is that water flowing down to the seas and oceans is only a part of the everyday cycle that plays itself out over and over wherever there is land.

Another part of the cycle is powered by the energy of our sun's radiation.

It evaporates all ground water and causes it to rise a few miles above the land into the air.

Winds created by the spinning of the earth on its axis, then carries the moisture in the form of clouds over the land and drops it again as rain around the entire world.

Depending upon the direction and flow of the winds, some places on earth get more water dropped on it than others.

Another factor that is important to us is that animals convert food and oxygen into carbon dioxide and water which adds itself to the above mix.

Plants themselves are powered by the light of the sun and convert free moving carbon dioxide and water into their food and oxygen that they eventually give back into the air, and is picked up by the winds, etc. Etc.

There are many more smaller cycles on Earth that are also mostly interconnected with life and moisture.

In every case, there must be an energy input to complete each of these cycles, and that energy input comes from our sun.

Since our sun is on hand with copious and abundant energy that has lasted for billions of years, and will last for billions of additional years more, we seem to have no problems maintaining the life cycles on our wonderful planet.

***

Ideas from the recent past still are around today, and those that had the deepest influences and touched most people, and resonated across most timelines, were the first ideas to be formulated.

Yet most histories of ideas ignore them.

Books on this subject usually start the story late with the invention of writing at the earliest, or with the great sages of the millennium before Christ.

So, the many ideas of our earliest ancestors are completely left out.

There are three reasons for this and all of them are bad.

First, people assume that the only knowable ideas are those that were written down.

But the error here is that most societies, for most of man's history, have highly esteemed oral tradition rather than later written ones.

Their ideas are inscribed in other ways—left in fragments of material culture for archaeologists to unearth, or buried deep in modern minds for psychologists, or they are preserved in later ages by traditional societies where anthropologists are sometimes able to elicit them.

Secondly, a vicious prejudice supposes that there are no ideas worth the name in the mind of the "primitive" or "savage," who is mired in prelogical thought, or retarded by magic or befogged by myth.

Thirdly, even some inquiries that are unprejudiced by contempt for our remote ancestors, tend to be misled by notions of progress.

The best thoughts, per this doctrine, are the latest, so the earlier material can linger in justifiable neglect.

In principal, there is no reason why people of the hunter-gatherer era should not have had ideas that anticipated our own.

There have been no known changes in human brain capacity since the disappearance 30,000 years ago, of the Neanderthals—whose brains, on average by most computations, were a little bigger than our own.

There is no evidence of any change in human intelligence over a very much longer period than that.

Maybe there was an era—much earlier—when life was poor, nasty, brutish, and short, and when hominids were scavengers without leisure for reflection.

But for hundreds of thousands of years, all people, as far as we know, were hunters and foragers.

Many of them enjoyed "stone age affluence": abundant game, high levels of nutrition, long days of leisure, unequaled in most farming societies, and plenty of time for observing nature and thinking about the observations that they had made.

Like all good jokes, the popular cartoon *The Flintstones* encloses a kernel of truth into their humor.

Palaeoarchaeologists date modern humans to about 40,000

years ago, "Cavemen" really were like us, with the same kind of thoughts that we have.

Anthropology can help interpret the material remains. Strictly speaking, there are no primitive peoples: all of us have been on the planet for an equally long time and all our ancestors evolved into something recognizably human an equally long time ago.

But some people have more primitive thoughts than others. This does not necessarily mean more simplistic or more unscientific thoughts, just thoughts that occurred earlier.

Societies closely in touch with their earliest traditions, are most likely to preserve their oldest thoughts.

We can therefore check archaeological finds against the evidence of the most traditional societies that survive in today's world, those that still live exclusively by hunting and gathering.

The fact that hunter-gatherers today have certain ideas, does not mean that people of similar cultures anticipated them tens or hundreds of thousands of years ago, but it raises the possibility and helps make sense of the archaeological evidence.

Mature cultures, which a lot of digs yield, offer a real clue to what goes on in the mind.

You can make informed inferences about a people's religion, morals, politics, or their attitudes toward nature and society, by looking at what they eat, wear, and use to decorate their homes.

No other evidence is as good as written evidence, but most of the past happened before writing was invented and it would be an unwarrantable sacrifice to foreclose on so much history.

At least in patches, we can clarify preliterate thinking by careful use of such evidence as we have been given.

***

In science fiction, experience seems to show that long stories have a definite advantage over short ones.

INTRODUCTION

The longer the story, all things being equal, the more memorable is the tale.

There is a reason for this. The longer the story, the more the author can spread himself out within it.

If the story is long enough, he can indulge himself in plots and subplots with intricate inter-connections.

He can engage in leisurely descriptions, in careful character delineation, with thoughtful homilies and philosophical discussions within the story.

The writer can play tricks on the reader, hiding important information, misleading and misdirecting them, and then bring them back to forgotten themes and characters at the right moment.

But every worthwhile story, however long or short, always has a point that is trying to be made.

The writer may not consciously put it there, but it will be there.

This, then is our following story. No tricks, no games, and only what we hope will be an interesting and well plotted out storyline.

Hopefully you will enjoy our efforts on your behalf.

This storyline has been in the back of my mind for many years.

***

And before I forget, I need to make this point.

Every once in a while, people speculate about the possibility of some cosmic catastrophe destroying life on our earth.

In fact, the movies are full of such things these days, and I personally, as a ghost writer, have contributed some of the way-out plotlines.

But is such a thing really likely to happen to us?

After all, life has existed on earth for well over 3 billion years, and nothing has happened to us so far.

Why shouldn't this peaceful existence continue?

But, that existence has not been entirely peaceful.

On several occasions, there seems to have been wholesale extinction of many different types of species.

The most recent occasion, and therefore the best preserved in the fossil record, took place about 70 million years ago, at that time, large reptiles that had ruled the earth for 150 million years, died out completely.

The dinosaurs, ichthyosaurs, plesiosaurs, and pterosaurs vanished.

Other less glamorous animals also vanished.

In fact, as many as 75 percent of all animals then living, may have become extinct over a comparatively short time.

As for the 25 percent of animal species that survived, they may not have done so by only the narrowest of margins.

It is not difficult to imagine that at the height of "the great dying," some 90 percent of all individual animals may have died and completely disappeared.

But why?

Scientist have striven to find an answer, and there have been all sorts of theories.

Perhaps the shallow seas drained away as the continents uplifted, killing off many species that depended on the ecological balance of such a sea.

Perhaps a certain kind of plant life died off, setting off a domino effect on animal extinction.

Perhaps the climate changed sharply for some reason.

Perhaps a nearby super nova drenched the earth with cosmic rays at a time when the planet's magnetic shield was either weak or absent.

Can we ever know?

There seems to be a strengthening view that a small asteroid, several miles wide, collided with the earth 70 million years ago, adding a thin film of iridium poisoning to the earth's surface.

The collision would also have kicked up scores of cubic miles of gravel, dirt and dust, so filling the stratosphere that for perhaps many years, very little sunshine could reach the surface.

Most of the plant life would have died off, and most of the dependent animal life with it.

The net result was that the earth was almost completely sterilized.

To be sure, that same event might happen again, but we know of no asteroid on such a collision course, so we don't really expect a repeat in the near future.

If one ever wanders our way again, we will simply have to figure out a way to blow it up or change its course away from us.

Nothing to worry about as far as I can see.

***

This is my final update on scientific comments.

I read the *Los Angeles Times* daily newspaper and always pay special attention to the scientific comment section.

There is an article written by the times scientific reporter Amina Khan with a most interesting report on individual stars (suns), that do not belong to the normal galaxies that were thought to include every known star within them.

She is stating scientifically that there are stars (suns) out there beyond the galaxies we normally look at.

Her findings tend to support my basic premise of visitors coming to us from beyond the normal galaxy configuration.

The date of her *Los Angeles Times* article is November 7, 2014 and is quite timely.

***

AS MANY AS HALF OF ALL STARS RESIDE OUTSIDE OF GALAXIES, STUDY FINDS

by Amina Khan Contact Reporter

Even stars can get lost in space.

Scientists who shot a rocket up beyond Earth's atmosphere for a matter of minutes have made a remarkable discovery about the diffuse background light that permeates the universe: As many as half of all stars may have been stripped from their home galaxies and flung into the darkness of the cosmos.

Astronomers were aware that some stars were intergalactic orphans. But the extent of the dim diaspora, reported in Friday's edition of the journal Science, came as something of a shock.

"I did not expect it to be half the stars — I thought that most stars would be in galaxies," said Harvey Moseley, an astrophysicist at NASA's Goddard Space Flight Center in Greenbelt, Md., who was not involved in the research. "It's almost like they're hiding."

The new information could compel scientists to reevaluate their theories of how the universe formed the galaxies we see today.

"If you want to understand what's happening in the formation of galaxies, you can't just look at the galaxies," said study coauthor James Bock, an experimental cosmologist at NASA's Jet Propulsion Laboratory in La Cañada Flintridge. "You're missing about half the light if you do that."

When astronomers study, the light coming from Andromeda, our nearest galactic neighbor, stripped stars seem to contribute less than 5% of the galaxy's total light, said Karoline Gilbert, an astronomer at the Space Telescope Science Institute in Baltimore who wasn't involved in the research. As a result, scientists haven't paid much attention to them.

Now it's clear they can't ignore them anymore. "There is still a large number of stars we aren't accounting for," she said. "We can't ignore orphan stars."

Scientists will also need to reevaluate the true boundaries of the fuzzy halos surrounding galaxies, said Michael Zemcov, an astronomer at Caltech in Pasadena and the study's lead author.

Astronomers have long wondered about the origins of the diffuse light permeating the heavens, which they call extragalactic background light. Earlier work with NASA's Spitzer Space Telescope had revealed a strange, splotchy background in infrared light, and scientists struggled to find a source.

One theory held that the faint radiation might be coming from the first primordial galaxies in the early universe during a critical epoch known as reionization, when the cosmos was only a few hundred million years old. Though not as ancient as the cosmic microwave background radiation that originated moments after the universe's birth, these galaxies are still old enough to elude detection by astronomer's telescopes.

Another theory proposed that the extragalactic background light might be coming from closer, more contemporary stars that were ripped from their homes when two galaxies smashed together.

To find out whether either theory might be correct, scientists with NASA's Cosmic Infrared Background Experiment sent a small telescope beyond the edge of the atmosphere to take clear shots of the sky in wavelengths of near-infrared light. From the resulting images, the CIBER team subtracted all the near-infrared light coming from the known stars and galaxies. What remained were the fluctuations in the background—which the researchers confirmed using data from the Spitzer telescope.

But in the long wavelengths of infrared light that Spitzer observes, it's difficult to distinguish primordial light from more recent light. So, the CIBER scientists looked at much shorter wavelengths of infrared light, just below the visible range.

If the background light was primordial, they would only find it at longer wavelengths, because the light would have been stretched out over time. But if the background light was coming from more recent sources, it would show up at shorter wavelengths too.

Sure enough, the background light was detectable even at the shortest infrared wavelengths they studied, Bock said. In fact, it seemed to gleam even more brightly at these shorter wavelengths.

That's a sign that the light was coming from more nearby stars in the universe — stars that hadn't been accounted for among the known galaxies.

These stars are so distant and faint that there's no way to pick them out individually, Bock said. They could only be detected by looking for this collective glow.

In fact, there's just as much background starlight coming from these dim rogue stars as is produced by all of the galaxies put together, the scientists calculated.

Exactly how many rogue stars there are remains unclear, and the answer depends on what types of stars are out there, Bock said. So, although they produce half of the background light in the universe, their population could potentially be markedly smaller than that of galactic stars.

But now that astronomers know what to look for, Moseley said, there could be hints of these hidden stars buried in the data already gathered by current telescopes, just waiting to be found.

Read the original article here:

http://www.latimes.com/science/sciencenow/la-sci-sn-half-stars-galaxies-rogue-universe-light-background-ebl-ciber-20141106-story.html

Los Angeles Times   LATIMES.COM

AN ARTIST'S conception shows galaxies surrounded by halos of free-floating stars. Astronomers were surprised to learn that as many as half of all the stars in the universe reside outside of galaxies.

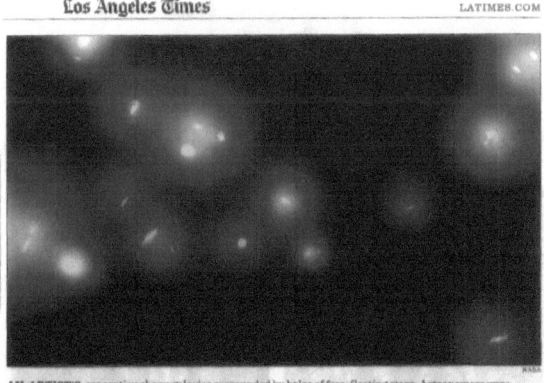

Is there intelligent life elsewhere in the universe?

PART ONE

COMMENTARY, VIEWS, AND RESEARCH

CHAPTER ONE

SOME HISTORY

An alien invasion is undoubtedly as old as humanity is itself.

Human hunting groups must occasionally have encountered each other, if only by accident, in their normal day to day living.

Any group not known to the other side was considered alien or unknown.

Each side must have felt that the other was invading their territory.

The obviously weaker side would have to leave, and if the solution to the immediate problem was not obvious, then there might have been threats made, or even a brief struggle to settle the problem.

We have the recorded history of many early civilizations that were suddenly overrun and replaced by raiders who soon settled into these newly acquired locations.

Probably the best and possibly the most recent example of our cultural ancestors being subjected to the horror of unexpected invasion, was as recent as the year 1240.

It was in this year that the Mongols of Ancient China, short and squat, swept into Europe on their small, but hardy desert horses.

Europe knew absolutely nothing about them, and had no way

of knowing that they were on the way towards them.

All that they knew, was that a huge mass of these fierce and terrible fighting men, moving with incredible speed and organization, were winning every battle, as they quite easily smashed through Russia, Poland and Hungary.

They were just turning their attention toward Germany, Italy and France, when they suddenly stopped fighting their many battles. Everything, in one amazing moment, came to a complete standstill.

As suddenly as they came, they turned and raced back eastward, as they tore apart Bulgaria in their haste to depart the area.

They started racing home as soon as they had heard that their great king, called the Khan, had died back in Mongolia, and they had to be there for the election of a new successor and leader.

If the King of the Mongols had not died when he did, then the world as we know it today, would be a completely different place.

It is a sure thing that nothing the Europeans could have done would have been able to stop them or even slow them down.

But leave they did and as history tells us, they never bothered to come back.

Instead of turning their attention to foreign lands, the new King, who they called Kublai Khan, (well known to us in the true story of Marco Polo, who kept a fabulous written journal about his travels eastward), turned his newly acquired army inward, and they concentrated on the complete conquest of all of China.

And so, the mighty Mongols were the last of the "alien barbarians" to storm against Europe in the Thirteenth Century, and foreign invasion was a thing of the past from China.

Now the only thing that the European's had to deal with were other European's, and this, as it turned out, was just as bad if not worse than the Mongols.

With Kublai Khan's soon to be completing his conquest of all of China, it allowed for peace between the Orient and their European counterparts.

Direct communications between these two parts of the now known world, became quite common, and China shared many of its wonderful inventions and creative ways with their neighbors to the West.

This was probably the biggest mistake that they would ever make.

Things such as printing, the magnetic compass and most of all, gunpowder, soon found their way westward from China to Europe.

For some reason, which never became clear, China never followed up on extending the capabilities of its inventions.

It left all the advancements up to the amazing Europeans, who made full use of gunpowder and other explosives.

Within a hundred years of the opening of China, "the tides of invasion" were reversed.

The "civilized Europeans" with their newly produced cannons, guns and ships of the line, soon fell on the coastlines on all the continents of the world including the Orient.

They eventually penetrated the interior regions of all far away locations, and ultimately Europe came to dominate the world politically, militarily, and as it does even today, culturally.

But the question that I wish to bring up, is to ask, "how did the non-European's feel about all this?"

How about the Africans who watched the Portuguese ships come from nowhere, and carry them off as slaves: the Asians who watched Portuguese, Dutch and English ships come in, set up trading posts, skim off most of the profits and treat them as inferiors.

The Native Americans who watched the Spanish ships come in and take over everything as they destroyed their civilization, were not very pleased with what was happening to them by persons that were alien to their culture.

All invasions, however, at least of the kind I am discussing right now, were all being done by human beings against other human beings.

However strange that the invaders must have seemed, Mongols to the Europeans, Spaniards to the Incas, etc. they were all clearly human beings interacting with each other.

Then there were also non-human types of invasions.

Rats, Locusts, the Plague Bacterium of the Middle Ages, the Aids Virus, Etc. Etc.

These and more do fall outside my subject matter for this introduction into non-terrestrial beings, and are going to be left out of the discussion and following story line.

Let me take a huge leap and go a step further by discussing intelligent beings, who were not human and in fact not earthly.

This possibility did not seriously arise until the time when it was thoroughly recognized that the planets were actually other worlds, and that the universe might be full of other planets outside the domain of our own sun.

At first, other worlds were suddenly the subjects of what was called "time and space travel tales."

Human beings went to the moon in science fiction and other far flung areas outside our home planet, but in the early days, Earth never played host to foreign invaders or non-Earthly visitors.

In the year 1752, the French satirist Voltaire, wrote several stories in which visitors from one of the planet Saturn's moons, paid a visit to Earth. It was a boring tale and nothing else of real interest was ever written up to that time about an invasion of our home planet.

But then, in the early 1800's, there was the discovery of thin, dark markings on our nearest neighboring planet Mars, which of course is located right here in our own Solar System.

These markings were interpreted by Percival Lowell, an American Astronomer around 1890, as being artificial waterways that were built by intelligent beings trying to use the ice of the polar caps of Mars to maintain some agriculture on their increasingly drying out planet.

He wrote several books on the subject that created quite a worldwide stir at that time.

The British science fiction writer, H. G. Wells, proceeded to make good use of the notion of life on Mars, and in 1908, published his famous book called "The War of The Worlds," which laid out for all to see, an alien invasion of Earth for the very first time.

I have always thought that H. G. Wells, in addition to wanting to write an exciting storyline with an unprecedented plot line, was also bitterly satirizing and picking on the terrible expansion ways of all Europeans of his time.

In the year that he wrote his famous book, the British were in the forefront of extreme colonialism, and he tried to show his fellows how being invaded must have felt by those actually being invaded.

Nothing however, stopped the British in those days.

Wells' novel created a new genre or storyline for others to follow.

The invasion of Earth by off-world being's, became quite popular fiction for many years.

People looked carefully at the way Wells made his invading Martians out to be non-sensitive exploiters of humanity.

Local critics were often comparing them to our own Europeans of that day.

However, there is no reason that I can come up with, to think that we will ever be invaded as a planet by outsiders.

As far as our best scientific minds know, no invaders have ever reached our planet, and for a variety of reasons, it might be argued that none ever will.

And, if however, that they one day do come, even though the idea is very "far out," there is no reason to suspect that they won't come in complete friendship and curiosity, to teach and to learn.

Yet, such is the power of humanity's own shameful history, that I, along with many others, doubted the wisdom or stupidity of sending plaques and recordings placed on rocket probes that were designed to leave our Solar System.

They were designed to leave us behind and go wandering off into interstellar space, in order that alien intelligence (if any), might find them, and then learn that Earthmen do exist and exactly where we live.

Many of us consider this a dangerous thing to do.

Why advertise our existence?

Why encourage possible ferocious aliens to come here to our Earth to possibly ravage and destroy?

Here then please find the story of what my personal thoughts and research have provided us in regards to evidence that we might already have been visited, and that we have been quietly observed and prodded with not the very best of intensions in mind.

CHAPTER TWO

We have all been hearing these stories since the early 1950's

This was the time when science fiction writers (myself included), jumped on the band-wagon and wrote all those stories to excite our readers and stimulate large numbers of book sales.

We were having a wonderful time creating storylines about flying saucers and people being abducted by aliens who would then implant things in human bodies.

Here now, is the first of my two-part novel of which part one is a real science story, and part two is a made-up science fiction story.

The difference is a science fiction story is always based upon things that are scientifically correct, but has a make believe and truly creative storyline, none of which is true.

Part one is the science story that I am about to tell you. It is not from my imagination, and is not made up in any way.

It is a true-life story, my true-life experiences, where-in I name real names, real organizations and real events, that I Bud Seligson, personally participated in.

I truly state, that to the best of my knowledge, everything is accurate and detailed to the point of my best memory and recollection of people, names, events, dates, etc.

My name is Bud Seligson, and I have been a ghost writer and story doctor to Hollywood for the past fifty years or so.

Most of those years have been fascinating, but a lot of them have been boring, boring, boring.

If my name sounds familiar to you, it is probably because you are aware of my science fiction novels of Leonardo da Vinci's time travels called Da Vinci's Clock and the novel that will be coming out shortly called *Nostradamus: A Science Fiction Kind of Story*.

This is my first attempt to write a story about events that personally brought me into direct contact with unbelievable meetings, locations, beings and events that made no sense to me at the time, and still has kept me wondering today, if what I thought happened around me, really did happen.

Let me back up a bit and go into a logical time-line of events and happenings that brought me to where I am today, sitting quietly at my computer, trying to organize my thoughts so that I could intelligently relate this unbelievable story and the follow up novel about aliens.

I would like to open with a little background and name six United States former sitting Presidents, who had acknowledged having to deal with classified documents about Unidentified Flying Objects (commonly known as UFO's)

1). President Harry S. Truman - born 1884 and died 1972. Thirty Third President of the United States from 1945 to 1953.

President Truman had the most control of all the following Presidents in terms of keeping secrets.

He was specifically identified as having full knowledge of the many Roswell, New Mexico incidents which will be discussed in greater detail further on into our story.

2). President Dwight D Eisenhower - born 1890 and died 1969. Thirty Fourth President of the United States from 1953 to 1961.

There were many stories and rumors that President

Eisenhower had an extraterrestrial meeting in 1954 at a private location.

3). President Lyndon B. Johnson - born 1908 and died 1973. Thirty Sixth President of the United States from 1963 to 1969.

He was invited to sit in on the secret meetings that were held upon the famous Kecksburg Crash Site.

4). President Richard M. Nixon - born 1913 and died 1998. Thirty Seventh President of the United States.

It was reported on several occasions that he showed alien bodies to famous comedian Jackie Gleason.

5). President Jimmy E. Carter - born 1924 and is still living. Thirty Ninth President of the United States.

President Carter has been quoted as saying that he had his own personal UFO sightings.

He helped start the Freedom of Information Act so as to give the world access to classified UFO information.

6). President Ronald W. Reagan - born 1911 and died 2007. Fortieth President of the United States.

In many of his speeches, he made references to aliens and several times confirmed extraterrestrial beings to Hollywood's famous director Steven Spielberg.

Now that we know that everyone from the top leaders of our country down to the average citizen is fully aware of the term UFO, and has an opinion about them, let us discuss the who, what, when and where of UFO's.

The excitement about unidentified Flying Objects began in the early part of the year 1947 and is still with us today.

Does the name Ken Arnold bring up any special memories for you?

The most common answer to this question is, "I never heard of him."

But the Ken Arnold name is very familiar to UFO investigators, who credit him with the first ever reported official sighting of what he described as an Unidentified Flying Object.

That label caught on, and ever since anything that was different or thought to be unusual in the skies above us, would be called a UFO

It was a very proper name for a catch-all of anything that we could not identify as something "earthly".

It didn't take very long for the Ken Arnold alleged comments about his seeing UFO's to sweep around the entire world.

As soon as the news stories appeared, reporting that Ken claimed to have seen airborne objects that flew just like a "flat dish or saucer," other people began reporting that they also had seen similar saucers.

I find it to be of interest and a curious development since Ken Arnold never said that the objects looked like saucers.

What he was quoted as saying was that "they skipped across the water just like a saucer would if someone threw it across the lake."

This difference of actual wording from Ken Arnold, was completely lost in the public's imagination and the UFO's thereafter were always saucer shaped.

Soon sightings of "saucers" were pouring in from around the country and from around the world.

Great waves of UFO sightings occurred in 1947, 1949, 1952, 1965 and 1973.

With the benefit of hindsight, we now know that the last large-scale national wave of UFO viewings, occurred in the Fall of 1973 and then suddenly stopped completely.

Might I suggest that after twenty-five years of sensational sighting reports, which ultimately led to absolutely nothing tangible, that if extraterrestrial visitors were really here, they must have gotten tired of us and departed in 1973.

My personal conclusion must be that if they were here, left us and have returned, then there must be something they either want from us or there is something that they want to tell us.

I believe I have some firsthand evidence that gives some real credibility to the above idea that there is something important that they want to share with us.

Please follow me as I attempt to make a clear position that "There Are Aliens Among Us."

CHAPTER THREE

Side bar by Bud - A brief discussion upon authors - H. G. Wells and Edgar Rice Burroughs, who are two of my all-time favorite writers.

I have always thought that H. G. Wells, in addition to wanting to write an exciting science fiction story with an unprecedented plot and story line, was also bitterly satirizing and criticizing the various countries of Europe in the late 1890's.

As previously touched upon within this project, it was noted that at the time of his writings, Europeans with the British in particular, had just completed dividing up Africa without any regard at all for the people living there.

This was an outrageous thing according to author Wells.

Within his story line about the Martian invasion, he tried to show the British how it would feel to have advanced intelligences treat humans as callously and as bad, as they themselves were treating the Africans.

Well's popular novel created a brand-new line of stories to follow - tales of alien invasions.

The way in which H. G. Wells made the Martians unpitying exploiters of humanity, was exactly what some of our fellow humans were doing to conquered nations.

I remember very well hearing my dad talking about the great hoax and scare that the famous actor Orson Wells brought to the entire world, when he did a radio station dramatization of H. G. Wells' *War of the Worlds*.

Dad told me that the programming was done so realistically, that people were rushing out of the big cities, and going into the countryside to escape the attacking Martians, who were said to be attacking the major population centers of the planet earth.

As I exit my brief thoughts on H. G. Wells, I should explain that he did something that no one else had done before.

He told the narrative about an unnamed hero and his brother who were trying to escape the Martian war machine in southern England in the first-person narrative.

In the first-person narrative, means that the hero tells his story as he is living each moment and just talks out loud as he moves about.

This was something new to science fiction where the person would say "I saw this and I saw that." It sounded to the untrained listener as if the hero was looking at whatever he was describing right on the spot, and it made it real for them.

If I wore a hat, which I don't, I would take it off in a salute to H. G. Wells, for doing something so real for the first time ever, and causing a panic in the streets where people ran out screaming about being invaded from the planet mars.

Finally, a movie based on his book, *War of the Worlds* which had the lead role given to the great Gene Barry, can still be seen here and there.

But the remake of *War of the Worlds* with possibly my all-time favorite action hero, tom cruise, gets my vote for possibly the best science fiction movie based upon a novel, ever done.

If I were asked to pick the best of all-time action hero's, my vote would go to Mr. Cruise.

And speaking of voting, of which I am, there is one more giant in the science fiction writer group who *must* be mentioned here.

You probably know him best for his "Tarzan of the Apes" series of books and movies, but I know him and love him for his special writings about the planet mars.

Of course, I am talking about Edgar Rice Burroughs, who was born in 1875 and died in 1950.

Edgar was born and raised in my home town of Chicago, and he spent his last few years in the city of Tarzana (California) which was named in honor of his world-famous character, Tarzan.

Edgar Rice Burroughs created the most interesting character in the world of science fiction in my opinion.

This great character was so unknown, that when I went to see the movie named after this character of his, I found myself sitting in a theatre with two other movie goers who were entirely unknown to me.

This movie did terrible with the unknowing public, and the movie studio had to write off the movie as a multi-million-dollar loss.

The world at large considered that movie about my all-time favorite sci-fi character, *John Carter of Mars* as a failure, but to me it was the best of the best coming to life on the big screen.

John Carter of Mars, was written in 1912, and it combined otherworldly adventures with elements of classical myths, fast paced plots and cliff hangers that were unbelievable.

It was based on *John Carter of Mars*, that I started my own humble sci-fi career.

Good, bad or indifferent, I really love this guy because he taught me to feel the clanging of a good sword fight, to listen to the cries of damsels in distress, and the guttural gesticulations of warriors locked in dire combat.

I cast all my hero's in the epic mold of *John Carter of Mars*.

Of course, I seemed to have sort of wandered off from my topic of aliens, but I wanted to share a few of my heroes with you.

So, I must get back to my story line of *There Are Aliens Among Us*. I wish to draw your attention to the next chapter where I will get back to business.

—Bud Seligson

FEB 25 2009

From left to right: Bud and Diane Seligson, and cousins Caren and Ed

18th Annual International UFO Congress Convention & Film Festival
February 22-28 2009
Laughlin, Nevada

Bud Seligson

18th Annual International UFO Congress Convention & Film Festival
February 22-28 2009
Laughlin, Nevada

Diane Seligson

Ed Grimsley's

NIGHT VISION

UFO
WARS

DVD
VIDEO

"Objects in Earth's Space Shooting It Out"

ABSOLUTELY **EVERYONE** WILL BE HERE.

JULY 2-5, 2009 ☿ ROSWELL, NEW MEXICO

FEATURING

RECREATION AND FAMILY ACTIVITIES AT CIELO GRANDE PARK JULY 4 - 5	**MUFON** SPEAKERS CONFERENCE & WORKSHOPS	FREE UFO 101 WORKSHOPS FOR PUBLIC
GALACTIC VENDOR MARKET		PLANETARIUM SHOWS DAILY RMAC
FILM FESTIVAL	**JEFFERSON STARSHIP** IN CONCERT JULY 3	COSTUME CONTESTS FOR HUMANS AND PETS
MAGIC SHOWS		AMAZING MAIN STREET PARADE JULY 3
ALIEN ATTRACTIONS	**MARVEL COMICS** SPIDER-MAN, CAPTAIN AMERICA & IRON MAN	

1-888-ROS-FEST ☿ UFOFESTIVALROSWELL.COM

CHAPTER FOUR

THE 18TH ANNUAL UFO CONVENTION
IN LAUGHLIN, NEVADA

I was invited to attend a very special convention in Laughlin, Nevada on February 22; 2009. Laughlin Nevada is about a two and one half hour ride from Las Vegas.

I was told that I was invited because I had gained a nice reputation as on open minded writer of unusual stories for many years prior to that invitation.

I knew that the real reason behind someone picking up the cost of rooms and meals for my wife Diane and I, and cousins Caryn and Ed, was to convert us into believers of the UFO thing.

I was told that there were hopes that I would write the adventures we were about to have for a magazine or two that I would later learn about.

I invited my favorite three people to join me for an all-expense-paid few days of doing something different and hopefully interesting there in the desert.

Up to that time, all I knew about Unidentified Flying Objects, was that in a remote desert place called Roswell, New Mexico, the United States Army was supposed to have removed a crashed UFO from a nearby location called Kecksburg.

The "Roswell Incident" is often held up as the best documented case of alien visitation.

It involved the alleged crash of an alien craft in Roswell, and the purported government cover-up of the debris and alien bodies.

Something admittedly did crash in the desert near Roswell, but I always thought that this something was not from outer space.

The accepted theory of the day, was that it was something launched from Alamogordo, New Mexico as part of a top-secret project called the "Mogul Project," in which the United States was attempting to spy on the Soviet Union's nuclear tests by positioning microphones and camera's high in the atmosphere on a series of huge floating balloons.

After a few years, Roswell, New Mexico was the most fascinating place to go.

It was featured on magazine covers, provided the basis for several films and television shows and was synonymous with aliens and UFO's.

The City of Roswell, took advantage of the popular notions and its once a year annual festival attracted well over 40,000 free spending tourist and investigators to the city. This went on for many years.

A special science fiction channel project also promised that hard, scientific proof of aliens at Roswell, would be revealed, but all that they were able to deliver was an empty archaeological dig.

The people living in and around Roswell still claim that the army did create a cover-up of gigantic proportions.

These eye witnesses said that they watched from a distance, as the army packed up everything that was lying on the ground within the impact area.

I noted in the article that I read, that the only true eye witnesses never called the crashed aircraft a flying saucer.

They only saw something that was broken up lying on the ground, and they had no specific knowledge of what it was that was lying there.

The army had keep all onlookers about a mile away, and they made the area a no-entry zone, and so, up to this very day, no one other than army people, had ever been seen going into or out of the closed off area.

There was sworn testimony that the local neighbors, with the use of small telescopes, could see dozens of large army vehicles carting off the broken parts of what looked like aircraft parts that they had picked up off the ground.

Everyone heard later, by whispers and rumors, that everything that was picked up that day, went into an army camp designated on the map as Area 51.

And repeating myself here in order to make a point, the army released a news bulletin the next day, saying that a large and highly secret weather testing balloon had crash landed in the State of Nevada, and that it was being sealed off for National Security reasons.

Prior to my coming to the Laughlin, Nevada convention, I never gave these incidents much thought.

Roswell, air balloons, flying saucers, and Area 51 were not in my awareness.

This complete lack of knowledge on my part, soon was about to undergo some major changes shortly.

When we checked into the hotel, we found out that we were the guests of a famous Ufologist (this means a self-appointed, private person looking into the field of UFO sightings), named Dr. Roger K. Leir.

When I later looked up Dr. Roger Leir, I found out that he had an impressive history and reputation within the scientific community.

Several weeks earlier, and before I knew anything about the convention that I would be invited to at this later date, the three of us, Dr. Leir, Dr. Tirsch, and myself, had met for lunch and discussed many things, but I don't recall the topic of UFO'S and their sightings or crash landings being brought up at that meeting.

And so, at the front desk of the convention, and much to my surprise, I found out that the same Dr. Leir that I had casually been introduced to by our mutual doctor friend, was one of the featured main speakers.

I began to realize THAT I WAS BEING SET UP, but by who, and what reason why, was still a mystery to me. I do love a good mystery and here I was not reading about one, but I was actually involved in the adventure (whatever it was), in a personal way. It was great fun and I couldn't wait for things to begin happening.

Of course, I explained all of this to my three companions and we all promised to keep our eyes and ears open and to enjoy the options that were opening. We were loving it.

Dr. Leir was written up as one of the main speakers at the convention, and the article went on to say that he was one of the world's most important leaders in physical evidence involving the field of Ufology. Very interesting.

The article further said that the good doctor was a podiatric surgeon (just like my friend Dr. Jerry Tirsch) in private practice for over forty-three years at this time.

I wish to point out that I suddenly was feeling somewhat uncomfortable noting that my new acquaintance, Dr. Roger K. Leir, and my dear friend Dr. Tirsch were both practicing the exact same kind of physical medicine on the ankle and lower foot.

When I had lunch with both doctors earlier that month, I did not think much about it when they told me that Jerry Tirsch had assisted Dr. Leir on several surgeries. I remember saying that it was nice that they could work together in the same medical profession. I didn't know that there was more to the story than that they were just working together.

I went to the internet and found out that both doctors had been written up as having performed surgeries that resulted in the removal of alleged foreign objects from several surgeries that they had performed.

I thought that it would have been proper for them to tell me where this was all going at the time of our lunch meeting, and not having to be surprised with my quick investigation. I later found out that this was their plan all along.

The internet gave me further details on Dr. Leir and I discovered that he, and his surgical teams (my friend Jerry being included in this group of surgical assistants) had claimed to have done fifteen surgeries on alien abductees (people who claimed they had metallic implants placed within their bodies by aliens).

I later found out that most or probably all of those who made this implant claim, were members of an exclusive and very interesting organization called MUFON.

I will have more to say about MUFON, because a few months later, I got Diane and I invited to one of their private meeting, and to a movie that they were showing. That evening was another fascinating one. I really love this stuff and was having great fun with all of this.

To go on with my Dr. Leir, Dr. Tirsch, and the convention, I do remember immediately making a telephone call to my friend Dr. Jerry Tirsch.

He confirmed that he had absolutely assisted Dr. Leir in what he called the famous 12th SURGERY CASE.

He told me that when I returned to Los Angeles, he would show me an actual film taken on the day of the 12th SURGERY.

He told me that the film would show the actual removal of an alien foreign implant in a human female.

Dr. Jerry said that he had the laboratory report and an actual sample of the foreign implant in his possession, and that he would share them with me when next we met.

He asked me to keep an open mind to all the various things that would soon be going on around me.

He said to listen to what everyone said, and to be neutral in my attitude as an observer and reporter.

Dr. Jerry told me that he had been the maker of all the arrangements that I found waiting for us, and he did it so that I would have a better understanding of the dialog that he and Dr. Leir wanted to open up with me on Aliens.

My friend sounded like a true believer and I agreed to stay neutral and to pay close attention to whatever came my way. I said I would advise my three companions to do the same.

We said goodbye, and I sat there for a few minutes reviewing our conversation. I knew that I needed to share all of this with the rest of my party, and I thought over lunch would be the perfect moment.

The four of us settled down at the coffee shop for a late lunch. I carefully repeated my telephone conversation with Dr. Jerry and showed everyone the literature that described Dr. Roger Leir who we now knew as our secondary host.

I'm not sure if we finished our food or not, but suddenly a very friendly young man, without being asked, pulled up a chair and squeezed himself into our table and sat between Diane and Caryn.

He was smart enough not to sit next to cousin Ed, who I jokingly refer to as Big Ed.

Big Ed belongs to cousin Caren (Diane's cousin) and he is the friendliest of cowboy's (Big Ed is the hero I wrote about in one of my cowboy stories called "Big Ed.")

Now Ed stands at six foot two before he puts on his three-inch heeled cowboy boots which takes him to a massive six-foot-five. He is no one to mess around with, and when our intruder placed himself between our girls, I had to give him a sign to back off before he threw whoever he was, over one of the tables just for the fun of it. As you can probably tell, Big Ed, is one of my favorite people.

Our intruder made his own introduction and did it with a big boyish grin on his face.

CHAPTER FIVE

Ed Grimsley introduced himself to all of us at the dining room table, and his open and friendly manner made for a very pleasant few minutes while the five of us got briefly acquainted.

He said that I was pointed out to him, and that he had a special invitation for all of us to attend something of great interest.

He said he had to excuse himself for about twenty minutes. He was in the middle of an important conversation when he saw us finishing up our meal.

He didn't want us to leave the restaurant before he could come over and introduce himself to us.

He asked if we would allow him to finish the discussion that he was having with an associate. He promised to be back as quickly as he could.

While he was gone, he asked if we would read the write-up about him in the convention magazine which he left with us. He said the article would explain who he was and what he had in mind.

Caryn opened the International UFO Magazine that he had left with us and started to read the article that was there next to his picture on one of the pages of the magazine.

She commented that his being on page three of the eighteen-page magazine, showed that he was pretty important to the organization.

We all continued to finish up our desert as she read the following article to us:

ED GRIMSLEY AND THE U F O WARS IN THE SKY

Ed Grimsley has been seeing battles between unknown aircraft in the night skies since he was a teenager.

Ed sees what appears to be "delta" shaped and saucer shaped aircraft in space, shooting at each other, using what looks like laser weapons.

He has seen hundreds of these objects recently, and in order to see them clearly, he uses military-grade, night-vision binoculars.

Many people have come to his night visitations, and viewed the objects shooting at each other on the edge of our earth's atmosphere.

With the use of his night vision glasses, even skeptics who thought that he "was seeing things," have now been convinced that what Ed Grimsley has been trying to tell people about all these years, is very real.

***

None of us really understood what it was that the article was trying to tell us, and so when Ed Grimsley returned and sat with us again, it was Big Ed, who put a few questions to him.

However, we were not able to get any type of answers from him that made any sense to any of us.

He saw that we were not getting what he wanted us to understand, and he went on to say that everything would be cleared up if we all would join him as his guest this evening at eight o'clock at the top of the Laughlin water supply dam.

He said that Dr. Roger Leir and several of the other speakers would also be there.

He left us with four small flashlights, and said that they would be needed in order for us to see where we were walking once we got to the dam.

There were no lights on the top of the dam, and in the darkness, people have been known to have fallen down the two-hundred-foot drop to the bottom.

This was kind of scary and quite different, but since we were here to explore all aspects of the convention, we agreed to stop up at the top of the dam at eight o'clock to see his show in the night sky.

In the meantime, we had several hours to kill, and Diane and Caryn headed for the hotel's gift shops, and Big Ed and I agreed to sit in on a few lectures that seemed interesting.

There were six lectures that were being offered that afternoon that Ed and I thought sounded interesting.

Since we had a limited amount of time, we each selected the three that most interested us.

With a promise from each of us that we would take extensive notes so that when we had free time, we would review what we heard with each other.

Here is a sample of some parts of the three lectures that I sat in on.

Each one took a good position on the topic they were discussing, and I must admit that I still think about some of the premises that were presented.

I still ask myself, what if, etc., etc.?

As follows are the highlight of one or more of the lectures that I sat in on.

My favorite lecture, also known as lecture number two that I attended, advertised something like this:

The question on the poster board that was outside the lecture room caught my eye and drew me in to listen. I am glad that I did.

The poster board read as follows:

OUT OF ALL THE PLANETS IN THE UNIVERSE, WHY IS OUR PLANET EARTH GETTING THESE UFO VISITATIONS? COME ON INSIDE WHERE THIS QUESTION WILL TRY TO BE ANSWERED.

***

There were two male lecturers who shared the stage and as follows is the information that I wrote down about what they had to say. I found it most interesting:

Many, many hundreds of thousands of years ago, a space ship that was one of many sent out to explore the far distant planets from its home world, was passing near to our sun, when it developed engine trouble and had to land on the most habitable planet in its planetary system.

Before they crash landed on our planet, they were able to send back to their home base which was many star years away, a distress signal which we would call an SOS.

They explained about their engine trouble, gave their planetary coordinates and asked for a rescue mission to come and get them.

The story continued saying that the several men and one woman aboard the ship did crash land and all survived but the ship was so torn up that they were forced to leave the wreckage of their ship behind them and set up a camp nearby so that they could wait out the arrival of their rescue party.

The problem was that the rescue party never came and they had to live out their lives on the planet earth.

The area where they finally settled after wandering

around the planet for many years, was a perfect area for human habitation.

With all of their advanced weapons, they had no problems with the wild life that was all around them.

There were no highly intelligent life forms on the planet and they were never in danger from the animal life that they tamed and used for food.

They probably took the space ship apart and took parts of it with them on their travels. They most likely used some of the living quarters for their rough housing and lived in the area where they finally agreed to settle into for generations with their children.

And speaking of children, it was obvious that the three men and one woman were able to bring forth enough offspring to populate the planet. They had many hundreds of centuries for their descendants to spread out over the planet.

For want of a better name, the area where they settled down was later called the "Garden of Eden" and the survivors became known as the collective "Adam and Eve."

And here is the kicker to their lecture that caught my interest. They thought that many, many, many generations had passed until the home planet had received the S O S with all the coordinates as to where the original starship had crash landed here on earth.

The lecturers said that they believed that the home world finally responded to the call and sent out another ship to come and see what happened to their fellow early explorers.

Naturally the crew of the newly arrived spaceship had the same human forms as the earlier crash-landed crew, and when they arrived they observed that the world was populated with people who looked just like they did.

After all they all originally came from the same planet, didn't they?

The speakers said they arrived in what we Earthlings called UFO's and that they were here to see how things turned out for their long-lost family members.

Now this interesting theory touched me in a curious way.

I did not believe or disbelieve their story that we are all related to the original crew that crash landed here on earth.

But it gave me a "writing spark," that inspired me to write a "quickie" story about the crash landing of our ancestors before I left the lecture hall.

I moved over to a far corner of the now empty room and wrote the following few hundred words about how I believed this theory might have unfolded.

Before this writing, I have never gone back to my notes that the lecture inspired me to write.

I found that the few pages fit nicely into my intended storyline and toyed calling it either:

1.   ADAM AND EVE ON THE PLANET EARTH
2.   WE CAME FROM ELSEWHERE
3.   THERE ARE ALIENS AMONG US

Obviously, I took number three as the title for this writing and I used my notes as an introduction for the story line that follows my personal experiences that I am sharing in this novel.

I used almost word for word the following notes that I made that day in the hotel's lecture hall for my story line in the novel that follows.

Here are my notes, exactly as I wrote them on that fun filled day, so very long ago:

***

The ship was alone.

She was moving, and moving fast, but there was nothing around her to show her speed.

She seemed suspended in a featureless universe of gray, transfixed in an empty fog, beyond time, beyond understanding.

There were no stars, no planets, no far galaxies like milky jewels against the shadowed velvet of space.

There was only the ship, and the grayness, and that was all.

The high, irritating hum of the atomic motors that were powering the distortion field filled the ship. Something was going wrong.

A door slid open and the navigator stepped into the cabin.

He was erect as always and quite calm.

Everyone's attention was on him as his strange black eyes swept around the room showing concern.

"We're going to be coming out of the distortion field and back into the regular universe in a few minutes," he said, "Better strap yourselves in."

"The distortion field still acting up?" The geologist asked.

"Some, yes."

"There won't be any ... Trouble ... Will there?" The only female member of the crew asked?

She was nervously wiping her hands on an overly fancy handkerchief as she threw out the question that was on all of their minds.

The navigator shrugged once again, "Better strap yourselves in," he said.

He pointed at the chemical engineer and motioned for him to follow him out of the cabin and head for the engine room where the captain waited.

The ship shuddered again. Somewhere in the walls a cable began to spark and hiss.

The gray emptiness around them seemed very near, pressing in on them, suffocating them.

The lights dimmed as they all sat there waiting.

And then the ship came out of it.

When it happened, it happened all at once. There was absolutely no transition as the ship blinked out of nothingness and entered back into normal space, back into a darkness where the stars were gleaming islands, and no wind dared blow.

It was a much friendlier place somehow, than the emptiness of inner space.

And that was because they were back in the universe that had given birth to the men and women of their far-off-world.

It was a familiar universe that was far easier to understand than the nothingness of inner space that they had just left.

Their ship continued to swim through the depths at close to the speed of light, but there was no sensation of movement, and the stars maintained their cold remoteness.

"Looks like we made it," one of them whispered to break the terrible silence, "That was a rough pullout. I think we were in real trouble there for a minute."

The sound of the atomics dwindled to a steady throbbing hum.

It was a sound that they all suddenly found to be very comforting.

CHAPTER SIX

I finished up my writing and left the empty lecture room and joined the hundreds of people milling about in the open central area.

It was time to take myself into the second of the three lectures that I had promised Ed that I would sit in on.

If this number two lecture was as interesting and stimulating as the first one, then I was in for another treat.

There were about thirty people already seated when I settled down into the back of the medium sized lecture room.

I saw most of the same people who were with me for the first lecture. I guess everyone made the same run.

I spread out in the back of the room and had several of my pens and yellow pads ready to go.

There was only one speaker this time, and she caught everyone's attention as she walked up to the speaker's table and slowly looked around the room.

This was a very pretty young lady that I would guess was in her early thirties.

She was well dressed and very well put together. I knew that even in the back of the room from where I was sitting, that even if her lecture was a waste of time, watching her deliver it would be worthwhile.

The topic of her lecture, as listed on the outside advertising board, was as follows, and the clever way they put it was what brought me in to listen:

"THE PROS AND CONS OF THOSE WHO CLAIM TO HAVE HAD AN OUT OF BODY EXPERIENCE"

Normally I would not waste my time on this topic because I thought that people who claimed that they saw a light at the end of the tunnel, was kind of boring when everyone always seemed to say the same thing after they had a near death experience.

"They saw a light at the end of a tunnel and their grandparents or some other favorite family member was waiting for them, and as they drew closer and closer down that tunnel, they stopped their forward movement and went backwards in that same tunnel, and before they knew it, they woke up back in their own body from which they said they had left only a few minutes before.

I must have heard this story with minor variations a dozen times and it did not hold my interest any more.

What I really came in for, was to buy a copy of the lecture that they were selling for ten dollars.

My friend Jerry Tirsch had told me not to miss seeing the cute young lady that he knew would be giving the talk. He told me to pick up a copy of the tape so that we could talk about it when I got home. He said the concept was a little bit different and would be of interest to the two of us.

The young lady made an excellent presentation and afterward I purchased the tape and I later found out that Jerry was right and it was something of interest.

I transcribed it when I got home and made a copy for Jerry. I have written out the main thrust of the tape and pretty much got it together in the speakers own words. Please read the following with an open mind and note that I neither accept or reject the concept of this out of body idea.

***

The following lecture was transcribed and is presented by Bud Seligson in its almost original narrative:

He was free of his body. He felt himself rising up.

But who was he? He was definitely more than a mere body, because that was the part of himself which he had just left behind.

The essence of his being had just floated away from his physical form.

He had no eyes, but somehow, he was able to see. And what he saw was himself, the human shape of himself, just lying there unmoving.

He seemed to be hovering at ceiling height and his eyeless gaze could focus right through the fighting armor that encased his body.

A few pieces of bronze had been torn away to reveal the flesh beneath his flesh. Or what had been his flesh.

What lay below was a corpse, a lifeless corpse, it was still almost entirely covered with the armor, but he could see through the bronze, see the emaciated body beneath.

The figure was dead. There was no doubt about that. He was dead. But he felt no pain, not anymore.

He felt absolutely nothing because he no longer had any physical senses.

Instead, his senses were far more than merely physical. He was not restricted to what his human body could perceive.

His body was dead, but he was not. He was more than his body, so much more.

His essence survived, and that was the greater part of him.

It was the part that had existed before he was born, then had been "trapped" at birth—just as his physical body was now "trapped" inside that bronze armor.

Now his body was free of him, although it was too late to do it any good.

His liberation had finally killed his mortal embodiment.

But it had also freed his soul.

He gazed down at what had been an element of him for so long, the flesh and bones in which he had inhabited the material world.

He had now left this body without any regrets, as easily as he had once cast off a pair of unwanted shoes.

There was no longer any connection between his temporary human form and his true substance.

He moved on up, higher, passing easily through the arched ceiling of the room, higher through the solid rock, higher through the building above, higher through the roofs and attics and rafters and tiles, higher and higher, and then finally out into the open air above.

Far below, he could see hundreds, perhaps thousands of tiny points of movement. They were people as he had once been.

And as he had once been, they were of no consequence.

With the escape from his body, his memories had also been released.

He remembered other times and other lives. He truly remembered what had come before.

With the escape from his body, his memories came flooding back. He remembered everything.

To be continued?

—Bud Seligson

CHAPTER SEVEN

After I had made my purchase of the lecture tape from which you had just read my interpretation of the transcript, I caught up with Big Ed at the restaurant, and we sat down for a meal and the promised sharing of our lecture adventures.

We took turns telling each other about what we had observed. Of course, I thought my thoughts were the more interesting but that was not important.

I spoke first upon the Garden of Eden lecture, and he told me about his first lecture which was on "Visitations to Early Man".

I thought that I might like to write a paper up on that. Cave drawings showing a possible human form in a space suit inside a cave, did sound interesting.

With my desert of vanilla ice cream and chocolate syrup, I told him about the pretty girl who spoke about "Out of Body Experiences."

He seemed more interested in hearing about the girl than about the lecture she was giving.

This is one thing that cousin Ed and I always agree on. A pretty girl should always be admired and talked about. This also held true about our good-looking wives, who fortunately were not with us at that moment as we discussed the lecture lady in great detail.

One of Ed's lectures was upon "Life on Mars" which he said was kind of boring.

We ended up talking about my favorite Martian, *John Carter of Mars*, which I have previously mentioned.

His third lecture was on Area 51, also a topic I mentioned previously.

I pulled a few lines from his lecture notes and report them as follows:

NO MAN'S LAND: GET ALIENATED ON THE Extraterrestrial HIGHWAY THAT LEADS TO AREA 51

Area 51's boundary line is at the edge of Nellis Air Force Base in the desert

The only place to spend the night along what is called the extraterrestrial highway, is a motel that has a tow truck holding up a flying saucer in its lift.

It is surrounded by signs showing pictures of an off-world creature and inviting earthlings in for a drink at the bar, a place to eat and a place to sleep.

I have made a copy of the picture Big Ed gave to me and it is on the following page along with a better picture for clarity.

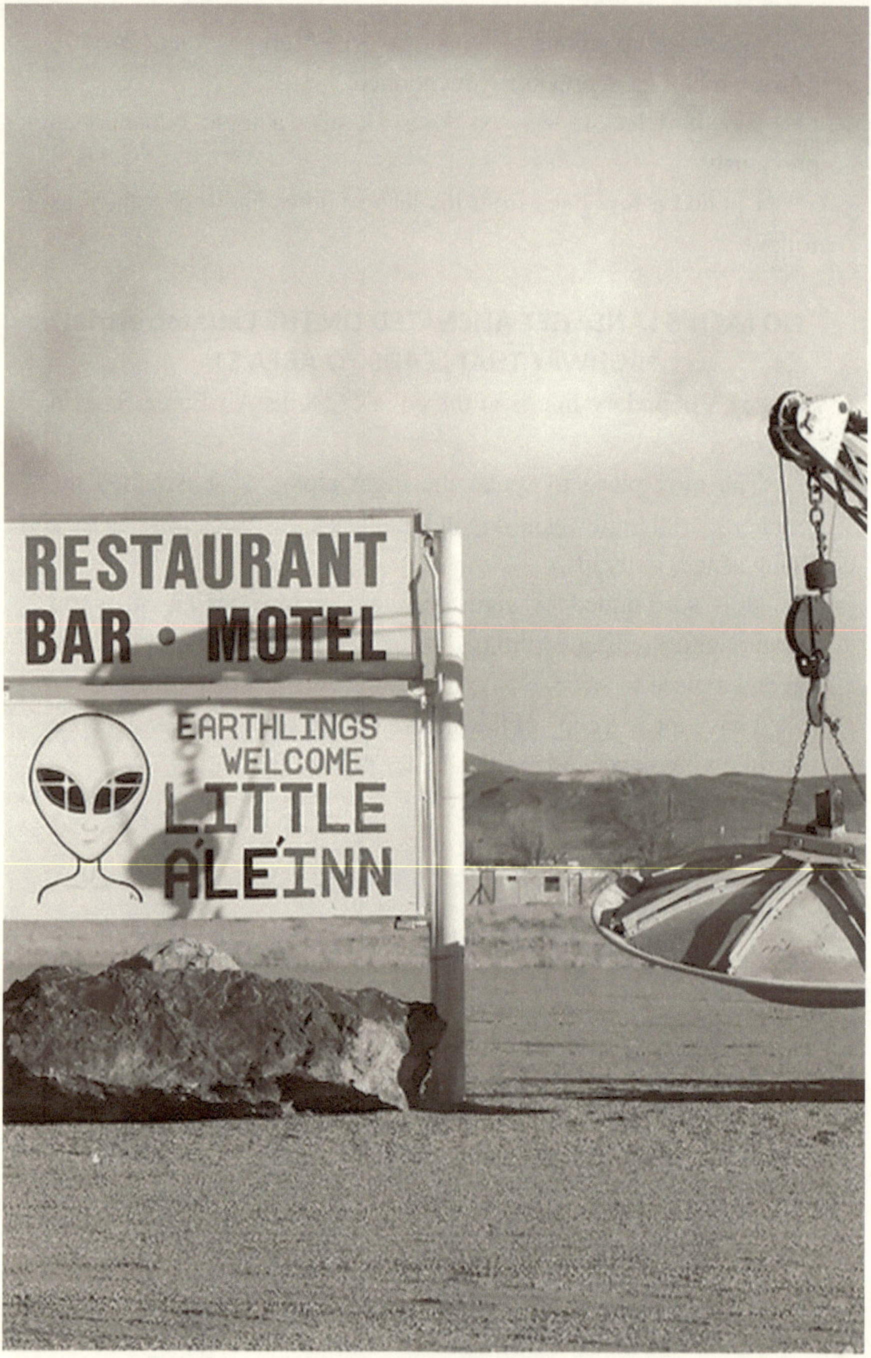
RESTAURANT
BAR • MOTEL
EARTHLINGS
WELCOME
LITTLE
ÁLÉINN

CHAPTER EIGHT

We both decided that we had listened to enough lectures and so we went looking for our wives to help us spend the rest of our time until we were to go out to the Laughlin Dam area to see just what Ed Grimsley's little adventure was all about.

True to our promise, we pulled Big Ed's car into the parking area at the top of Laughlin's Dam.

The dam supplied the water to Laughlin and all of the small Nevada communities in and around the area.

It was a wise move on the part of Ed Grimsley to have given each of us a small flashlight, because it was pitch black as we got out of the car.

It was a few minutes before the eight o'clock meeting time and, we followed several other people holding flashlights down a path that led to a large, flattened area.

This large area had seven or eight lanterns patterned into a circle and it was there where we all entered.

Dr. Roger Leir walked over for a minute and invited us all to kindly attend his eleven o'clock lecture in the main auditorium tomorrow.

He said that he would reserve four seats within the first few rows for us.

We agreed to attend, and we then turned our attention to Ed

Grimsley, who stood in the center of the lantern lit area.

Ed was speaking through a handheld microphone which was connected to a speaker. His voice came out a little squeaky but clear enough for easy understanding:

"Good evening everyone." Ed Grimsley's voice came at us all from the speaker.

"Thank you all for coming to what I promise you will be an evening completely different from any other evening you have ever spent.

Since everyone here has come by as my special guest, I would like to get started and not waste any of your time.

My assistants will be moving among all of you, and handing out united states government issued night binoculars.

I was only able to purchase twenty-four of them, so please be sure to turn them in when you leave.

Also, donations toward my expenses would be greatly appreciated.

What I want you to do when we are all ready, is to form a circle around me as I stand in the center of the loose circle of lights that we have created.

These lights will be turned down to an absolute minimum, so that they will not distract us with anything but their lowest brightness.

When you are ready and everyone's focus is on me, I will be pointing my handheld laser light to a special location in the sky that I want you to look at.

Please look exactly where I will show you with my light laser. I want you to concentrate on that specific spot using your binoculars at first and also, I want you to look at the same spot without the binoculars.

In this way, you will be able to assure yourself that the binoculars you were given, are not programed to show you something that is really not there.

Caryn and Ed, Diane and I, were standing close up together,

about fifteen to twenty feet away from where Ed Grimsley was centered.

The group surrounding him was absolutely silent as he pointed his laser light straight up above him into the night sky.

He moved the light around a bit before he ended up with it about a ten or fifteen-degree angle away from where we were all standing.

Without going into details and comments heard from the people around us, let me give a summary of the comments the four of us talked about when we finally returned to the hotel's coffee shop.

We intentionally did not talk about what we saw until we had settled in.

Here is what we all agreed upon:

We all had looked around at the night sky and saw absolutely nothing until we individually located the bright spot in the sky that Ed Grimsley had his laser light pointed at.

When we focused on that exact spot, we all agreed that there really was something there.

We agreed. That we saw three triangular shaped aircraft (which we later learned that Ed Grimsley call "delta's"), moving in a circular motion.

They were trailed by two additional triangular shaped aircraft in what appeared to be a formation of some sort.

We looked at these five objects through the night goggles and with our bare eyes.

The vision was very clear through the night goggles, and somewhat misty with the naked eye, but we all agreed there was something up there and that we all saw them with both goggles or the naked eyes.

We all remembered Ed Grimsley's voice in the background saying that what we were seeing, was secret government aircraft up there protecting our planet from unwanted visitors from outer space.

He said that the advanced technology that allowed us to put

those crafts up there, was developed from the information that we took out of the downed flying saucer that crashed and was taken to area 51 (as I had previously discussed).

The four of us were at a complete loss for words.

We knew that we had seen something, but just what it was, we did not know.

We decided to just put the evenings sightings behind us and go to sleep for the night. We really had a most different and exciting day of it and tomorrow was Dr. Leir.

Speaking for myself only, I will positively say that I know that I saw those five very distinctive aircraft moving about, but I have no idea what they were. They were too high up in the atmosphere to be the usual aircraft that we are used to seeing. Most interesting as my friend Sherlock Holmes would say.

I truly did see something moving around up there where there should have been nothing moving about at that altitude.

Was Ed Grimsley correct? Did our government really have aircraft up there defending our planet and if so, defending it from whom?

My head was spinning from all the questions we were asking and getting little if any answers.

CHAPTER NINE

Promptly at eleven o'clock the next morning, the four of us were seated in the third row, front section, off to the left side of the stage.

We were all set to listen to my new friend Dr. Roger Leir.

If you will recall, it was my longtime friend, Dr. Jerry Tirsh, who told me that he assisted Dr. Leir on what had been called the twelfth surgery.

Please recall that I was to meet with Jerry when Diane and I got back to Los Angeles after the convention, and talk to him about alien implants that he said he assisted Dr. Leir in removing from a female patient.

As follows, I am reproducing the advertisement promotion for Dr. Leir's lecture. I am quoting word for word from page 8 of the 18th Annual International U F O Congress/Convention and Film Festival.

The cover magazine is dated February 22–28, 2009, and it was, of course, being held at the Aquarius Hotel in Laughlin, Nevada.

The heading for the lecture was:

NEW STARTLING FINDINGS ON ALIEN IMPLANT RESEARCH:
A LECTURE BY Dr. ROGER Leir

Dr. Roger Leir is one of the world's most important leaders in physical evidence and research involving the field of ufology.

In this special session, he will reveal scientific proof that we are not alone.

Dr. Leir is a podiatric surgeon, in private practice for the past forty-three years.

He has written numerous books including *the Aliens and The Scalpel, UFO Crash in Brazil,* and *Casebook on Alien Implants*.

Dr. Leir and his renowned surgical teams, have performed many surgeries on alleged alien abductees.

These surgeries have resulted in the removal of many interesting objects that are suspected of being alien implants.

These suspected objects have been carefully scrutinized by some of the most prestigious laboratories in the world.

To name a few such as the Los Alamos National Lab, The SEAL laboratories, The University of Toronto Laboratories, and The University of California, San Diego.

The laboratory findings have been baffling and some comparisons have been made to meteorite samples.

In addition, several special tests have shown metallurgical anomalies such as highly magnetic iron, combinations of crystalline materials with common metals, as well as isotopic ratios not of our known world.

Dr. Leir has traveled to Brazil, and performed exhaustive research into the famous Varginha, Brazil case.

Recently he formed a 501-C Nonprofit organization for research purposes called A&S Research, Inc.

***

I made a lot of detailed notes on the lecture from Dr. Leir as well as tape recording everything that was said. I believe I picked up on the direction Dr. Leir was heading with his interesting comments and projections.

What I found extremely strange was that Dr. Jerry in Los Angeles. and Dr. Leir here in Laughlin, Nevada were talking about the same surgery which they both called the "12th Surgery".

I found myself more interested in what Dr. Leir was saying than any of my companions who sat through the lecture looking bored. The old saying of "different strokes for different folks," seemed to fit this situation.

***

Notes taken by Bud Seligson based upon Dr. Leir's lecture and a tape recording made by Bud of the session.

On September 23, 2006, Dr. Roger Leir and his surgical team from A&S research, recently announced that they have performed their twelfth surgery for the removal of a suspected alien implant.

Dr. Leir, a southern California podiatrist, is considered by many, to be the world's leading authority on alien transplant research.

Art Bell, world famous radio's *Coast to Coast* morning show host, made the following statement after interviewing Dr. Leir on his radio program.

Art Bell is quoted as saying, "Dr. Roger Leir did four hours on my open national airwaves show.

Much of what he said, sounded as if it should have been on a special need to know basis, but I got him to share his thoughts with the world exclusively through my program. It was quite an accomplishment for me and my network."

To continue:

Dr. Leir is the author of seven books on the subject of unidentified flying objects, and has over three thousand hours of radio experience.

He has appeared on hundreds of television broadcasts worldwide.

The 12th surgery patient, was a female "abductee" in her early forties.

The object which was verified on x-ray, was located in the third toe of the right foot.

The patient had contacted Dr. Leir about three years prior, and had explained to him that she believed that she had an alien implant in her toe.

She was sent a special package containing one of the initial contact questioner's given to clients who suspect that they may be involved within the alien abduction program, designed by A & S Research.

Once the package was returned, she was asked to have another x-ray taken of the suspected area and then to have the x-ray sent directly to Dr. Leir for evaluation by his staff of radiologists.

The patient was very compliant and did exactly as she was advised.

Evaluation proved that there was a noted radio-opaque object in the third toe of the right foot.

This object measured approximately 6 mm in length (which is the approximate diameter of a pencil lead).

Once it had been verified that there was indeed an object present, further communication with the client continued.

She was asked many questions pertaining to her personal involvement with the subject of alien abduction, as well as the involvement of her immediate family.

She explained that there were numerous members of her family who had experiences involving extraterrestrial beings.

She also sent Dr. Leir a series of audio cassette tapes

that were made by her father, in which he talked quite freely about his own experiences.

During the following months, A & S research set out to acquire the funding necessary to perform the surgical procedure.

Once this fundraising was accomplished, a specific surgical date was set.

The following two pages show professional photos of the procedure and doctors Leir and Tirsch performing the surgery.

All photos for A&S Research by Micheal Portanova Photography

page 1 of 2

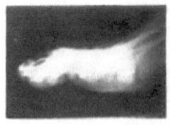  

A & S Research
9-23-2006
001.jpg

A & S Research
9-23-2006
002.jpg

A & S Research
9-23-2006
004.jpg

A & S Research
9-23-2006
005.jpg

   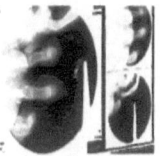

A & S Research
9-23-2006
006.jpg

A & S Research
9-23-2006
011.jpg

A & S Research
9-23-2006
020.jpg

A & S Research
9-23-2006
029.jpg

A & S Research
9-23-2006
026.jpg

A & S Research
9-23-2006
027.jpg

A & S Research
9-23-2006
037.jpg

A & S Research
9-23-2006
045.jpg

CHAPTER TEN

The following few pages are notes I took based upon a delayed meeting with my friend Dr. Jerry Tirsh, and from the final statements made to me in a final cup of coffee meeting I had with Dr. Leir the same day after his lecture had ended.

Since the client was local to the southern California area, her stay near the surgical site was not a terrible inconvenience to her.

Her immediate recovery was quite satisfactory, and she was allowed to go home the next day after the procedure had been performed.

Earlier, when the patient had arrived at Dr. Leir's surgical office, she immediately had additional x-rays done to the toe area, and she was re-examined and made ready for the surgery.

The x-ray showed that the object had moved slightly from its original position and had wedged itself into one of the toe joints.

This movement resulted in the metallic object breaking itself up into three separate pieces.

Dr. Leir and his assistant Dr. Jerry Tirsch, knew from reading the new x-ray, that the three-piece removal instead of a one-piece removal would slightly complicate the upcoming surgical extraction.

At this time of the scheduled surgery, several expensive instruments were being rented for use in detecting electrical and/or magnetic energies that might be coming from the object still within the toe.

The doctors used a simple gauss meter, a magnetic stud finder, and a radio frequency detector, which resulted in the following findings:

There was a positive reading of 6 mil-gauss detected on the gauss enter, and the stud finder isolated the exact spot where the object was imbedded in the soft tissue.

The amazing thing both doctors told me at different times, was that there was no entry marks or cuts on the outer skin of the subject.

And when I asked the question as to how something from outside the body could get into the body without making a mark on the skin that they were passing through, I received no response.

The doctors themselves were amazed that something could be implanted without making a scar on the covering tissue. This was another question that was to go on unanswered.

The radio frequency detector was very precise as it homed in on the exact spot of the implant.

When pointed directly at the third toe, there was an active reading of a radio vibration (a radio signal like a person would get when turning the dial to change radio stations). How or why this happened also went unanswered.

The surgery was performed under local anesthetic and a C-arm x-ray device was used to help locate the tiny object that was surrounded by so much body tissue.

As with other surgeries performed by Dr. Leir, the singular object had broken into three separate items.

When these separated items were removed, they were found to be attached to live nerve tissue.

The soft biological surrounding tissue in the toe, was also removed at the time of the surgery to keep things as intact as possible for later examination.

Again, as with all previous surgeries, numerous individuals witnessed the live procedure.

Each person present was said to be prominent in the field of UFO studies.

My inquiry into the names of who was present would not get answered by either doctor.

I thought that not wanting to give up the names of those who observed the procedure to be extremely secretive and unprofessional. I kept my opinion to myself but I still wonder why names of observers were never given.

Were they just. Regular humans like the doctors and myself, or were they a little bit more?

I never did get an answer and I found this also to be a bit strange. Why record the procedure and ask a writer like myself to write up the goings on and then deny answers to questions? Something did not add up.

Also, the studio of Michael Portanova photography, took still photographs and a full video of all the procedures, but when I requested copies, I was denied. This was getting stranger and stranger.

I later learned that the tissue and metal objects were all sealed in a container after they were immersed in the patient's own blood serum.

This was to avoid shocking the samples by taking them out of the blood fluid they were used to being in.

I was told that after a certain amount of time, the data from the lab testing would be given to the Leir/Tirsch team.

At a later date when I asked for a copy of the test results, my request was once again denied.

I remember at the time (many weeks later) being upset again and taking all my notes and papers and putting them away where they have remained for all these years.

I told the doctors at this later date, that I could not and would not write a story for them in that I was not being given the true facts.

My understanding is that since I would not do the story, they could not get anyone else and so until now, nothing has been done with the events that I have been telling you.

It appears nothing about any of this and the following further events that I shall be describing, ever was put into print until now.

And now to continue with the time line.

***

Dr. Leir concluded his lecture and I left the lecture room and found an empty room nearby and wrote up my notes. As you know I like to immediately record my thoughts after detailed lectures like this, so that time does not remove some of my memories.

CHAPTER ELEVEN

The next morning I was on the telephone with my good friend Dr. Jerry Tirsch, who confirmed everything that was covered by Dr. Leir in his lecture yesterday.

Jerry said he had pictures and analysis reports to give proof to all the claims being made about the 12th surgery.

We set up an agreeable time for just the two of us to meet into next week.

I was really discouraged, and by now quite doubtful, if there really were scientific backup materials to show that there was a surgery performed upon this person of whom they claim had an alien, radioactive artifact within her body.

Diane, Caryn, Big Ed and I were just finishing breakfast when our new friend, Ed Grimsley came over to say goodbye to us.

Ed Grimsley is a very nice fellow and talking to him was always fun and very different.

I said that I would keep track of his progress on the lecture tour that he was undertaking. I told him I would watch for his name in UFO things that would be popping up from time to time. Before he left he gave me his private telephone number and he told me to call if anything of interest came up. I told him that I would call. To date, I never made that call.

Today was getaway day for us, and while my three companions

went up to complete packing and get everything ready for the trip home, I wandered over to the see if anything of interest was still happening in the convention hall.

I listened for a few minutes to a lady who said she had a good friend who drove one of the delta ships (Ed Grimsley's night vision) back and forth to the underground cities on Mars. (I smiled to myself and moved on).

I spent a few minutes at a talk about how the speaker, while traveling through a remote mountain road in the nearby State of Utah, had his car stall out by an alien vessel, which he described as a flying saucer, flew overhead.

He said that when it flew out of sight, the electrical system on the car started up again and he went on his way.

He described the saucer in great detail and even had several beautiful sketches that he had made available for sale.

The electrical failure idea reminded me of an old science fiction movie that I had seen many years ago, I believe it was called *The Day the Earth Stood Still*. I quietly left the room and moved on.

The final item that I found interesting was not in a lecture hall, but was found in a properly bound article being passed out by a pretty young lady.

An article like this, that was based upon a lecture given by someone in the recent past, is called an "updated informative," and I always take the time to read these articles if I recognize the author.

In this case I was familiar with the name of Astronomer James McGaha, who was the director of the famous Grasslands Observatory in Tucson Arizona.

I was always impressed with the little I knew about James. I knew that he was a former pilot and retired U. S. Air Force Major and a longtime evaluator of Unidentified Flying Objects reports and claims.

He was also a scientific consultant to the Committee for Skeptical Inquiry (called the Skeptics Group). This group investigates all claims being made about anything claimed to be off-world.

I believe his handout article was interesting enough to be included in our discussion of Alien Things, and so I have reduced his long and a bit boring report into the following few paragraphs.

The article was called:

THE TRAINED OBSERVER OF UNUSUAL THINGS IN THE SKY

"Unfortunately, unidentified flying objects seldom if ever, come from anyone really knowledgeable in trained observation of the skies and unusual phenomena.

Nor do they come from those who really understand perceptual issues, and how beliefs and expectations can influence the interpretation of unidentified phenomena.

People often think that pilots and police officers are trained observers in these regards, but experience has repeatedly shown that they are not.

The writer of this article is an astronomer who has spent thousands of hours observing the sky, and is a retired Air Force C-130 pilot, and a longtime analyst of unidentified flying objects.

He is concerned with misunderstandings about what makes a good observer.

In his view, a good observer has the skills, knowledge, experience and ability to critically analyze what is being observed in the sky.

The observer has to observe without any prejudice, accurately record what was being observed, and be able to personally evaluate the data.

He has put together the following list of seven areas of expertise needed to be a profession observer:

1. Astronomy
2. Atmosphere

3. Aeronautics
4. Physics
5. Physiology of visual illusions
6. Human beliefs
7. Visual perception
End of report

CHAPTER TWELVE

Big Ed had the girls and the car all ready to go, and all I had to do was sign us all out at the front desk, and then we were on our way back to Las Vegas.

We spent a few fun filled days in the Las Vegas Casino's, left some of our money at the tables, ate well and saw a few great live shows at the hotels on the Las Vegas Strip.

Diane and I enjoyed being with our cousins, and loved the convention, but the best part of the ten days that we spent away from our home in Los Angeles, was getting back home again.

I had two things left to do before I could close up this storyline.

We had to attend a movie premier in Hollywood called *Moon Rising*, which was being given by an important group of UFO believers call MUFON, and I had promised a meeting with my friend Dr. Jerry Tirsch.

As you must have noted by now, that I always have my wife Diane with me on anything important to be observed.

Not only is she beautiful to me, and a wonderful person, but she is very smart and extremely observant.

Diane can sense a lie or an untruthful statement better than anyone I know.

I take her with me whenever something needs investigation. She is my Watson to my Sherlock Holmes, only much better looking.

The first thing to do here, is to define the who and what of MUFON.

MUFON is listed as an American nonprofit organization that investigates cases of reported UFO sightings.

It is one of the oldest and largest UFO investigative groups.

It was originally established and called "the Midwest UFO Network of Quincy Illinois.

It was established on May 30, 1969 by Walter H: Andrus, Allen Utke and John Schesslor.

***

Now that MUFON was known to us, I pulled a few strings, and got an invitation to attend their next meeting which was being held at an academy awards theatre in north Hollywood, California.

Diane and I got to the theatre early and had no problem with our credentials and admittance, and just like that, we were inside the exclusive gathering.

The only people out of perhaps three hundred guests that were dressed as normal theatre goers, was Diane and me.

At first, we thought that we were at a costumed ball because practically everyone was in a costume or semi-costume of some sort.

Diane and I are definitely extroverts, which means we can and will talk to anyone at any time.

We split up and worked the room for the hour and a half that we had until showtime for the special showing of their sponsored movie, *Moon Rising*."

We gathered ourselves together in about an hour's time so that we could compare our observations before we took our reserve seats in the theatre for the much talked about movie.

We agreed upon every single point which was astonishing, every person that we had talked to had the same basic answer.

It was as if they all had rehearsed together and got their lines given to them.

Question: What do you remember about being abducted?

Answer: It was all a blur and not clear.

Question: What proof do you have that this really happened to you?

Answer: My scars and bits of metal that are in my body.

Question: May I see a scar?

Answer: No. Not unless you are a member of MUFON, which I know that you are not because you are not wearing the neck identification piece.

Question: I am holding a small but powerful magnet in my hand. Can you place it on the skin outside your body where the metal inside would attract and hold it?

Answer: No.

Question: Were you the only person in your family abducted?

Answer: Some said yes and others said that another of their immediate family members was abducted.

Question: Is it a requirement that you have to be abducted in order to be a MUFON member?

Answer: No.

Question: Can you explain that a little fuller?

Answer: No.

***

We each gave up and met at our meeting place a bit early. As we started to go into the theatre, I recognized a face in line ahead of us.

It was George Noory from the Art Bell's famous *Coast to Coast* Radio Show.

It was Art Bell who had recently talked about having Dr. Roger Leir on his program.

I quietly asked Diane if she thought that George Noory was

abducted in order to be a MUFON member since he was wearing a neckband.

The only response I got from her was a blank stare as we continued to walk into the rapidly filling auditorium.

Within a short period of time, the lights dimmed and onto the stage walked Jose Escamilla who told the audience that he was the producer/director of the movie that we all were about to see.

He said that it was his belief that the space agency for the United States of America, was hiding aliens who had landed on, the far side of the moon, and that this was the base where UFO's worked out of.

We all know that the far side of the moon is never in full view from the Earth, because as the moon rotates in the night sky, it always keeps one side facing the Earth and the other side facing away.

Jose Escamilla's theory is that there is much to see on the other side of the moon, and by watching his movie which is next on the program, he would prove his position.

The lights dimmed and the movie which was a narrative by Jose, spoke about the truth being held away from all of us by our Government.

Jose spoke very well, and the pictures were snapshots that he said was real, but to my untrained eye, I couldn't tell real from unreal.

What they showed as bases with possible aircraft coming and going was not clear to me, and at the end of the showing we came away with the opinion that it was a nice movie, and we wished them well but it was not convincing.

We left the theatre and went out for coffee and promptly forgot all about what we had watched on the big screen.

Well, so much for the non-event with MUFON and the not-so remarkable movie.

What the last thing left on my agenda was, to move onto my appointment with my friend Dr. Jerry Tirsch who wanted to discuss alien implants.

By now, I was getting pretty tired of all the science fiction stuff, and I promised myself after Dr. Jerry, I would put all of this hocus-pocus science stuff behind me and do some regular story writing.

As a coincidence, I received a special delivery letter from Jerry which allowed me to avoid having a final meeting with him, at least that is what I thought at first.

I have made a word for word copy of the note he sent me:

HELLO BUD:

I just wanted you to know in advance of our upcoming meeting later this week, that I decided to come forward with information upon the 12th surgery when I acted as back up surgeon to Dr. Leir.

This surgery did take place at the private surgery center of Dr. Leir's on September 23, 2006.

There was a videotaping and many still pictures taken for the official record at the time of the surgery.

If more copies are wanted, I should be able to get them for you.

I have enclosed eight still shots that will be explained to you when we meet.

The picture of the two surgeons in hospital gowns show me on the left and Dr. Leir on the right.

You should be able to also see the film crew recording this historic procedure.

After you and I have our official visit, I am planning on entering into evidence, items to prove the honesty of my statements that the bits of metal that we removed from the subject's ankle area, vibrated in my hand and emitted a simple form of radio wave.

This radio wave gave off a signal that would allow whoever implanted it to be able to local the patient wherever she went.

I believe that it is only logical to assume that the intelligence who did the implanting, would want to follow the whereabouts of their homing device, and the radio transmitter was the simplest way to do something like that.

What I find the most interesting of all, is that the implant was performed, and the transmitter was placed under the skin, and connected to nerve endings, without breaking the skin of the patient.

In all the many years that I have been practicing medicine and doing surgeries, I have never come across anything like this before.

If my information, pictures, etc., etc. are well received, then I plan to come forward with more facts, pictures and other information as needed.

In closing, I wish to quote an old saying from our by-gone youth, (the 1950's of course):

I plan to simply knock your socks off!

Submitted in full and complete text
by Bud Seligson

 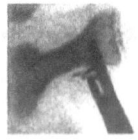  

A & S Research   A & S Research   A & S Research   A & S Research
9-23-2006   9-23-2006   9-23-2006   9-23-2006
056.jpg   058.jpg   063.jpg   064.jpg

A & S Research   A & S Research   A & S Research   A & S Research
9-23-2006   9-23-2006   9-23-2006   9-23-2006
070.jpg   075.jpg   078.jpg   095.jpg

CHAPTER THIRTEEN

I had my last meeting with Dr. Tirsch, and I believe that everything that he said to me was sincere, and that he truly believed in what he was trying to explain.

I also believe that all the other people like Dr. Leir and Ed Grimsley, completely believe in what they are saying.

I am sure that they have seen and done things that the rest of us can only speculate and dream about.

I, however, can't get my teeth into the Alien thing at this time, and so I am withholding my judgement for another time, and I plan to go no further with the topic once I finish up these concluding last few pages of the first of the two novels that I am combining into one larger literary piece.

***

MY FINAL STATEMENT ON THE ISSUE IS AS FOLLOWS:

Unidentified flying objects have fascinated the public, and both amused and frustrated science-minded skeptics since the late 1940's.

Please don't think that unidentified flying object are *passé*, or things out of the past, because they are not.

It is true that we do not seem to be getting great waves of mass UFO sightings anymore, but that proves nothing.

Those sightings started within newspapers and television news reports, and snowballed into what I once heard the great Carl Sagan jokingly refer to as the great UFO flap that being the technical term that is still thrown about every so often.

The media has since the early days, vastly multiplied, and the lines between news and entertainment have blurred.

What we have now are internet sites and dozens of episodes and multi-part series on cable television devoted to UFO's.

Too often the few cases that pop up are sensationalized, and old cases resurrected, and credulously picked through.

The UFO movement itself, keeps evolving, trying to find something new (crashed saucers, contacts, abductions, supposed cover-ups and conspiracies).

Within the last year or two, Larry King aired three consecutive Friday's of hour-long television shows, devoted to spreading beguiling misinformation to millions of viewers.

I am reserving my judgement until someone or something comes forward with something more concrete and believable regarding aliens and UFO's.

Respectfully,
Bud Seligson

CHAPTER FOURTEEN

I am closing with the following few pages of part one of the two-part novel that I have promised.

I enjoyed everyone and everything that I came in contact with putting part one together.

As follows please find a final article written about the 12th implant surgery that has come to be the most famous of all other surgeries to date.

The article is written by Sean Casteel and it appeared in one of the scientific journals dealing with the U F O phenomenon.

I am quoting the article word for word. Please read it in full as it sums up everything we have been saying up to now.

IS THIS THE "HARD" EVIDENCE SKEPTICS HAVE BEEN ASKING FOR?

by Sean Casteel

The search for physical evidence of UFOs, and their mysterious occupants, has been a long and fruitless one, endlessly frustrating those who believe but cannot prove their stories and accounts to others.

As haunted as this century has been by lights in

the sky, and small grey figures with large black eyes, no one can say beyond a shadow of a doubt, that the phenomenon exists at all.

But that may all be changing thanks to the work of "alien hunters" and UFO researcher Derrel Sims of Houston, Texas, and a medical doctor named Roger K. Leir of Thousand Oaks, California.

Their partnership has resulted in the kind of evidence that even medical and scientific professionals throughout the world can neither dismiss or ignore.

It all started in May of 1995 in Los Angeles at a conference called "UFO Expo West."

Derrel Sims was operating a booth at the conference and had some x-rays on display when Dr. Leir walked up and began a conversation with Sims that would eventually make history.

"I was displaying some of the x-rays," Sims said, "of people who had alleged implants.

"Dr. Leir looked at the implant x-rays and said that he wanted to see the radiology report that says that those three metal clips were noted in the soft tissue adjacent to the approximal phalanx of one woman's great toe.

"The problem I told him, was that there was no recorded history of the surgery."

Sims also told him that there were also similar x-rays of the subject's mother and brother as well, which serves to indicate that abduction may run in families and along genetic lines, as many researchers already believe.

Dr. Leir was so impressed with Sim's x-ray evidence, that he immediately offered to surgically remove the implants for free.

When a friend of Sims offered to fly two abductees from Texas to California at no cost as well, the deal was struck.

Leir assembled a medical team in Thousand Oaks, California, that consisted of fellow members of the Ventura Santa Barbara counties chapter of the Mutual UFO Network (MUFON) who were also medical· and psychological professionals, and the surgeries were scheduled for august of 1995.

Per Dr. Leir, both patients had abduction histories. The male had what we call a "screen memory."

He stated that when he was about seven or eight years old, he woke up in the middle of the night.

He lived on a small farm in Texas. He saw a bright light out the window and a voice calling him outside.

He went outside and then went into one of the fields and saw a light above a tree.

"From that light," Dr. Leir relayed the story, "there approached about a basketball sized light form and somehow he was told to reach out and grab that floating ball of light."

"Instead of doing that, he became frightened and turned to run back into the house. Then, supposedly the ball of light exploded, and he felt something hit his hand."

Like many abductees, the man forgot about the experience until many years later when he went to visit a chiropractor because of pains he was feeling in his arm and back.

The chiropractor asked him if he'd ever injured his hand or ever had hand surgery.

Of course, the answer to both questions was "no."

The chiropractor then showed an x-ray of the object that was clearly seen in his hand.

In later years, the man made the important connection with Derrel Sims, and he underwent regressive hypnosis, with the Texas researchers, and ultimately ended up on Dr. Leir's operating table.

This was the surgery labeled "the 11th surgery." The next surgery on the female patient was the now famous 12th surgery that we have been talking about in our previous writing of this novel.

Just like her brother, the female patient had an implant in her big toe.

All during this 12th surgery, the patient was given subconscious suggestions on healing her body.

The next day she walked out of the clinic unaided and on her own two feet.

After having the operation on Saturday, she was back at work on Monday with no ill effects. She never had the need to use crutches or other physical aids once the implants were removed.

For the sake of experimentation with hypnotic anesthesia techniques, Sims let the brother have only normal forms of anesthesia.

He healed up just as well, but it took nearly two full weeks to do so.

Sims feels the worthiness of hypnotic anesthesia is vindicated by this surgery.

"We wanted to see specifically," Sims said, "if there was a measurable difference in the two people in terms of their healing rate.

"Of course, one was seven times faster than the other one, in effect.

"That provided some interesting input and a possible direction we might want to go with some of the other people."

But back to the implants themselves. After Dr. Leir and his team removed the two implants from the toe of the woman, some surprises happened immediately.

"The implants were surrounded by a membrane," Dr. Leir said. "a very dense membrane.

"I've been removing foreign bodies for about thirty years and I've never seen anything like this"

"The membrane was so dense that you couldn't cut through it with a surgical blade.

"Extreme caution was then used in transporting the implants.

"There are many stories," Leir said, "about implants disappearing or exploding or turning themselves into powder.

"to be on the safe side, I felt the best way to transport these things was in the individual's own body fluids."

"we had our surgical nurse remove some blood from the patient and spin it down.

"we then removed the serum and the implants … with the membrane attached, and placed into the serum to transport them back to Texas.

Back in Texas, there were even more surprises in store for the group.

"After some preliminary tests were done," Leir said, "they did a fluorescence test using ultraviolet light.

"The objects fluoresced a brilliant, bright green.

"They were also highly magnetic.

"The membranes could dry out and when they were ready, they could be removed from the metallic substances within.

"The metallic substance within was a black metal that had a little bit of flakiness to it.

"It was probably some minor oxidation that had occurred.

"The objects were then sent to an engineer of

electronics, a chemical engineer, and for testing with an electron microscope."

Dr. Leir plans to publish the test results in several medical journals in hopes that other medical and scientific professionals will take an interest in the subject of alien abductions, and give the team's new found evidence an open-minded examination.

Understanding the objects may also hold a great deal of promise for human medical technology.

"It's virtually impossible," Leir said, "to poke something into your body without getting an inflammatory reaction."

"When you get a fresh injury, or an acute foreign body inside the body, you get an infiltration of inflammatory cells.

"That's true whether you get a sliver in your foot or a surgeon implants a screw into a bone to hold things in place.

"Everything will undergo inflammatory reaction if something is inserted that doesn't belong there.

"But, something different happened this time.

"I sent the tissue surrounding this encapsulated foreign body out to a lab," Leir said, and it came back with absolutely no inflammatory cells and no inflammation whatsoever.

"This was something never seen before and it seems to be something new to our world of medicine."

"This is a puzzle that will only be solved by the passage of time and discovery."

***

Please draw your own conclusions to all of the above.

And now may I please draw your attention to the novella that follows?

It is 100% science fiction and I hope you will enjoy it.

I call it *There are Aliens Among Us*

PART TWO

THERE ARE ALIENS
AMONG US

THE NOVELLA

THERE ARE ALIENS AMONG US

An original story
by Bud Seligson

INTRODUCTION

OPENING STATEMENT

In ancient times, people had a great deal of fun and excitement just imagining all of the strange plants and animals that might exist in the mysteriously distant and unknown regions of the world.

There were unicorns and sphinxes and dragons and giant birds and man-eating trees, and so on, and so on.

But by now we have filled up our world with so many people, that there are no more wide open spaces anymore, and it seems to hold no more mysteries for us to discover out there.

Before written history began, human beings had already tamed all the animals and plants that they were ever going to tame.

Cats, dogs, pigs, goats, sheep, cattle, horses, donkey's, geese, ducks, hens, grains, fruit trees, etc. Etc.

These and many more were all out there for our ancestors to make into our companions, and our slaves.

Most primitive animals and insects also have been put to use by us, as we plunder beehives for honey, and certain caterpillar cocoons for silk.

We can put yeast cells to work fermenting things for us) and we can do limitless other things with the world around us.

Human beings are pretty smart, aren't we?

***

"There is nothing more powerful than an idea whose time has come."

—Victor Hugo

"When you sit with a nice girl for two hours you think it's only a minute, but when you sit on a hot stove for a minute you think it's two hours. That's relativity."

—Albert Einstein–1938

***

WARP SPEED

Albert Einstein stated that it is not possible to travel faster than the speed of light.

The creators of television's *Star Trek* invented "warp speed" in which distances are compressed to allow spacecraft to reach their destinations faster than that speed of light.

I have chosen to go along with the writers of *Star Trek* and I shall be using the concept of warp speed within our storyline.

***

A WARPED UNIVERSE
THE IDEA OF EINSTEIN'S RELATIVITY

The Theory of Relativity is an outstanding example of an idea that changed the world by changing the way we perceive it.

In 1901, Albert Einstein was a second-class technical officer in the Swiss patent office.

He was stuck in a small office which acted as the containment of his genius.

He had been expelled from school as being disruptive, and suspected of arrogance at college.

Local jealousies had excluded him from an academic career, and buried him in complete obscurity.

But in the year 1905, he emerged like an underground worker from a mine, to detonate a terrible charge.

He produced a theoretical solution to an experimental paradox which was: when measured against moving objects, the speed of light never seemed to vary no matter how fast or slow the motion of the source from which it was sent.

If the speed of light is constant, as we know it is, then Einstein inferred, that time and distance must be relative to it.

He said that at speeds approaching that of light, time must slow down and distance shorten.

Einstein has yet to be proven wrong.

***

THE IDEA OF AN ORDERLY UNIVERSE

Early humans saw through the apparent chaos of nature: with a bit of imagination, and thereby, order was revealed.

Animals perceive relationships between events that matter to them: the death of prey and the availability of food, or worsening weather and the need for immediate shelter.

The urge to make sense of data by moving around and therefore accumulating information, seems to be a property of the mind, or what people loosely call "instinct".

There comes a point, however, when the "sense" we make of knowledge, transcends anything in our experience, or when the intellectual pleasure it gives us exceeds material needs. At that precise moment, an idea is born.

Once evolution endowed mankind with sufficient memory, people could observe patchy instances of order in nature, and make mental connections between them such as the regularity of the heavenly bodies, the progress of the seasons, and the predictability of the life cycle.

But that was only the scaffolding upon which the idea of an orderly universe was erected.

There is a huge gap for the mind to leap, between observations of orderly relationships and the inference that order is universal.

Indeed, the claim that order encompasses the whole of nature, is so counterintuitive, and so contrary to experience, that it must have originated as an idea.

Order is not visible, except in a few fragments, the rest has to be inferred from the clues of which Homo sapiens were quite capable.

***

THE IDEA OF MEASURING TIME

Since its first formulation, human beings have used this breakthrough idea as the basis for organizing action and recording experience.

Time is change.

No change, no time.

Change is observable, and you can measure changes roughly against each other, perhaps without having an idea of time. For example, to eluding a pursuer or to capture prey, or noticing that different lifeforms grow at different rates.

A universal standard of measurement is, however, an idea.

It arose, of course, from observation, from awareness that some changes—especially those of relative positions of celestial bodies—are regular, cyclical, and therefore predictable.

The realization that they can be used as a standard against

which to measure other such changes, transcends observation.

It was a perception of commonplace genius that occurred in all human societies so long ago, that ironically, we are unable to estimate a date for it.

It is a fair assumption that it happened in consequence of the relationship between the cycles of the heavens and other natural rhythms.

This is especially true of our own bodies, and of the ecosystems to which we belong.

Examples are the passage of the sun which matches intervals of sleep and wakefulness.

The moon's cycles coinciding with the menstrual cycle.

Species we eat, grow or fatten according to the season.

Hence, the choice of timekeeping's standard to clock all of these things.

Some human groups keep star time, usually on the basis of a cycle of the planet Venus.

But everyone we know of, usually keeps time using the solar day and year, and the lunar month.

It is a safe bet that keeping time by all of these means, is one of the oldest and longest enduring ideas in the entire world.

***

THE SIZE OF THE UNIVERSE

It was only in the 1920's that human beings finally began to get a glimpse of the true size of the universe.

Instead of thinking of the universe as a collection of individual stars, astronomers began to think of it as a collection of galaxies, and even of clusters of galaxies, and that helped them to begin to understand some matters much better.

For instance, there is no really accurate way of estimating the actual age of the universe by studying the stars of our close up milky way galaxy, but it could be done by observing the different galaxies.

It does not seem likely, however, that we'll ever know of any other universes.

We may be doomed to know only our own, which we now have traced back to what may be its absolute beginning, some 15,000 million years ago.

We also have predictions that there will be an absolute "ending" of the universe as we know it sometime in the future.

And with that statement the business of writing this science fiction story need to be done.

***

EARLY MODERN Homo sapiens
(THE TRUE HERO'S OF OUR FOLLOWING STORY)

All people today are classified as Homo sapiens.

Our species of humans first began to evolve nearly 200,000 years ago, in association with technologies not unlike those of the early Neanderthal man.

It is now clear that early Homo sapiens, or modern humans, did not come after the Neanderthals, contemporaries. But were their contemporaries.

Compared to the Neanderthals and other late archaic humans, modern humans generally have more delicate skeletons.

Their skulls are more rounded, and their brow ridges generally protrude much less.

They rarely have the occipital buns found on the back of Neanderthal skulls.

They also have relatively high foreheads, smaller faces, and pointed chins.

Homo sapiens (Latin for wise man) is the scientific name for the human species).

Anatomically modern humans first appear in the fossil record in Africa about 195,000 to 200,000 years ago.

Caveman is a stock characteristic based upon widespread concepts of the way Neanderthals or early humans may have looked and behaved.

Cavemen are portrayed as wearing shaggy animal hides, armed with rocks or cattle bone clubs, unintelligent, and aggressive.

This image of them living in caves arises from the fact that caves are where the preponderance of ritual paintings and artifacts from prehistoric cultures have been found.

In fiction, entertainment sometimes especially or satire, depicted as pure cavemen are as living contemporaneously with dinosaurs, a situation contradicted by archaeological and paleontological evidence which shows that dinosaurs became extinct 66 million years ago, at which time our ancestors were not yet in the mix.

Scientists have discovered a wealth of evidence concerning human evolution, and this evidence comes in many forms.

Thousands of human fossils enable researchers to study the changes that occurred in brain and body size, locomotion, diet, and other aspects regarding the way of life of the early human species over the past 6 million years.

Millions of stone tools, figurines and paintings, footprints, and other traces of human behavior in the prehistoric record, tell about where and how early humans lived and when certain tools and ideas developed.

The journey of mankind demonstrates the overwhelming importance of climatology.

It was always due to a window of opportunity (lower sea levels during glaciation afforded easy migration and so on).

There was a massive eruption of Mount Toba 74,000 years ago, which caused an instant volcanic winter and a thousand-year ice age.

Ironically, while this natural disaster not only decimated but also jeopardized mankind to the point of extinction, it hastened the development of prehistoric technology, which ultimately led to the occupation of previously inhospitable land areas as people constantly were on the move.

Humans are currently found throughout the world: in permanent settlements on all continents except Antarctica, and on most habitable islands in all of the oceans.

Anatomically modern Homo Sapien population was known from the middle east as long as 100,000 years ago, from east Asia as long as 67,000 years ago, and southern Australia as long as 60,000 years ago.

European fossils are known from only 35,000 years ago, and seemed to be late starters.

Humans are found in all terrestrial habitats worldwide.

Humans extensively modify habitats as well, creating areas that are habitable by a much reduced set of other species as in urban and agricultural areas.

With the aid of technologies such as boats, humans also venture into many aquatic habitats, primarily to obtain food.

Humans are an exceptionally diverse species morphologically.

Many aspects of size vary substantially with environmental factors such as nutritional status.

Historically there has been an effort to organize human physical variations into races, although there is no scientific basis for the application of a race concept to human variation.

Human physical variation is continuous, and available evidence suggests that gene flow among human populations throughout history has been the rule rather than the exception.

Humans are characterized by their bipedalism and their lack of significant body hair.

Males are generally larger than females, with more pronounced muscle development and generally more hair on the face and torso than females.

Human cultures are marked by a wide range of approaches to mating.

Childrearing in most cultures is accomplished with some degree of help and cooperation from other members of the group, including related and unrelated members.

Humans are capable of breeding throughout the year.

Gestation length is 40 weeks on average.

Typically, one young is born, although twins occur occasionally and multiple births rarely.

Interbirth intervals, birth weight, time to weaning independence and sexual maturity, all vary substantially with the nutritional status of mothers and the young, and are influenced by local cultural practices.

Human lifespans vary tremendously with nutritional status and exposures to diseases and trauma.

Humans can live more than 100 years: the longest-lived human that has been carefully documented, was 122 years old.

Most humans live to be 50 to 80 years of age, providing they are able to survive their most vulnerable childhood years.

Average life expectancy in many parts of the developing world, is from less than 40 to 60 years.

In the developed world, average life expectancy can be well over 80 years.

Humans are one of the most behaviorally, socially and culturally complex animal species. Ancient men were nomadic hunter-gatherers, but the development of agriculture approximately 10,000 years ago, revolutionized the way humans lived.

Agriculture ultimately led to increases in regional human population and concentration in urban centers, and dramatically altered the cultures, economies, and relationships among human populations.

In general, humans are highly social animals that are active mainly during the day.

Some human populations remain nomadic or migratory, while most live mainly in one general area.

One of the most notable aspects of human biology and evolution, is the extensive use of tools.

Early human populations constructed sets of specialized tools, such as chisels, and knife blades, from stones, bone, antler and ivory.

Human technological innovation is one of the most definitive human characteristics.

Related to this innovation, is the complex development of human art and symbolism, including written language.

Like most primates, humans use vision extensively in perception and communication.

Humans have excellent color vision, although limited. Visual acuity in low light is limited.

Humans also use sounds extensively. Human languages represent one of the most complex systems of communication in the animal world, and the diversity of human languages is astounding.

Touch is an important mode of perception, and it is especially important in close social bonds.

Humans have a moderately well-developed sense of smell and taste, which is used to determine the suitability of foods and discover information about the environments they live in.

The evolution of complex language is considered one of the hallmarks of Homo sapiens.

Archaic humans were capable of complex language, although Homo sapiens anatomy seems to have evolved to favor the production of complex sounds in anatomically modern humans.

Humans generally eat a highly variable omnivorous diet.

The components of diets vary tremendously with regional availability of foods.

Some human cultures restrict their diet to vegetarian ones, relying on plant sources of proteins.

Foods are often extensively prepared and stored away for future use.

The use of fungal colonies, such as yeasts, for creating cultured foods, such as beer, bread, and cheeses, is widespread.

The human primary diet consists of three basic foods:

1. Animal foods: birds, mammals, amphibians, reptiles, eggs, blood, body fluids, carrion, insects, terrestrial non-insect arthropods, mollusks, terrestrial worms, aquatic crustaceans, echinoderms and other marine invertebrates.
2. Plant foods: leaves, roots and tubers, wood, bark or stems, seeds, grains, nuts, fruit, nectar, pollen; flowers, sap or other plant fluids, and algae.
3. Other foods - fungus and microbes.

***

BEGINNINGS
THE OBSOLESCENCE OF MANKIND (OBSOLESCENCE IS DEFINED AS THE PROCESS OF BECOMING OBSOLETE)

About a million years ago, an unprepossessing primate, one of our early ancestor's, discovered that his forelimbs could be used for other purposes beside locomotion.

He also discovered that sticks and stones could be grasped and held in these limbs.

And then he came up with the idea that once these objects were grasped, they could be quite useful for killing game, digging up roots, defending himself from attack, and a hundred other tasks.

On the third planet from our sun which we call Sol, tools had appeared and the place would never be the same again.

The interesting thing about this is the fact that the first users of these tools were not men.

This is a fact appreciated only recently by our scientists.

Those tools were first used by pre-human anthropoids, and by these early discoveries, they doomed themselves to extinction.

For even the most primitive of tools, such as a naturally pointed stone that happens to fit the hand, provided a tremendous physical and mental stimulus upon these very early users.

He had to walk erect in order to use them, and no longer did he have use for huge canine teeth, since sharp handheld things could do a better job with less stress upon his jaw.

In order to use all of these wonderful new things, he had to develop a natural dexterity of a higher order which he quickly started to do.

These were the needs of early Homo sapiens, and as soon as they started to fill in these needs, the earlier models of humanity were quickly headed for the junk heap of history and rapid obsolescence.

***

ABOUT TIME

Man, is the only animal to be troubled by the concept of time.

From that concern comes much of his finest art forms, a great deal of his religions, and almost all his science.

This was because of the temporal regularity of nature—the rising of sun and stars in the darkened sky, the slower rhythm of the seasons (which led to the concept of law and order in all things), and to astronomy, the first sciences that mankind attempted to understand.

Changeless environments like deep oceans, or the cloud-wrapped surface of Venus, provided little stimulus to intelligence, because there was nothing to see, and therefore nothing to study.

It is not surprising, that those cultures which existed in out of the way regions of little climatic variation, like Polynesia and topical Africa, often had little conception of time itself.

Other societies, forced by their surroundings to be aware of the passage of time, have become obsessed by time.

Perhaps the classic example is that of ancient Egypt, where life was regulated by the annual flooding of the Nile river.

No other civilization, before or since, has made such a determined effort to challenge eternity, and even to deny the very existence of death.

Time has been a basic element in all religions, where it has been combined with such ideas as reincarnation, foretelling the future, and the interesting worshipping of the heavenly bodies.

Examples of these are the monolithic calendar of Stonehenge, the Zodiac, and the architecture of the ancient Maya Indians of Mexico.

It was only in the twentieth century that we learned a little something about the true nature of time, and were even able to influence its progress by nanoseconds.

Now we all know that time is neither absolute nor inexorable, and that the tyranny of the clock may not last forever.

It is hard not to think of time as an adversary, and in a sense, all the achievements of human civilization are small victories in man's ever ongoing war against time.

Whatever their motives may have been, the early cave artists were the first to win any gains over time.

About a thousand generations ago, when the mammoths and the saber-toothed tiger still walked the earth alongside our ancestors, they discovered a very intelligent way of sending not merely their bones, but some of their thoughts and feelings into the future.

We can look through their eyes, across the gulf of time, and see the animals and ideas that shared their world.

It is an interesting peek into the past.

***

GRAVITY

Of all the natural forces, gravity is the most mysterious and the most implacable of them all.

It controls our lives from birth to death. It kills us or maims us if we make the slightest slip up.

No wonder that conscious of their earth-bound slavery, men have always looked wistfully at birds and clouds, and have pictured the sky as the abode of the gods.

The very expression "heavenly being," implies a freedom from gravity which, until the present, we have known only in those dreams.

***

AGE OF PLENTY

The raw materials of civilization, as of life itself, are matter and energy, which we now know to be two sides of the same coin.

For most of our human history, and all of prehistory, only the most modest quantities of either matter or energy were used.

During the course of a year, one of our very remote ancestors, would consume about a quarter of a ton of food, half a ton of water, and very negligible amounts of hide, sticks, stones and clay.

All the local energy required was produced by muscle power, plus occasional small contributions from wood fires.

With the rise of technology, that very simple picture has changed way beyond recognition.

The yearly consumption of the average American citizen, is more than half a ton of steel, several tons of coal, and hundreds of pounds of metals and chemicals, whose very existence was completely unknown to science a century ago.

Every year, over twenty tons of raw materials are dug from the earth to provide each of us with the necessities and luxuries of life.

No wonder we hear warnings from time to time, of critical shortages, and are told that within a few generations copper or lead may be added to the list of rare metals.

***

SPACE - THE UNCONQUERABLE

To our ancestors, the vastness of the earth was a dominant fact controlling their thoughts and lives.

In all earlier ages than ours, the world was seemingly huge and wide indeed, and no man could ever see more than a tiny fraction of its immensity.

A few hundred miles—a thousand at most, was infinity.

Great empires and cultures could flourish on the same continent, knowing nothing of each other's existence except for fables and rumors as faint and far away as through from a distant planet.

When the pioneers and adventurers of the past left their homes in search of new lands, they often said goodbye forever to the place of their birth, and the companions of their youth.

Only a lifetime ago, parents waved farewell to their emigrating children in the virtual certainty that they would never meet again.

Those that they loved, would be almost as good as dead to them.

And now, within little more than one generation, all this has changed.

Over the sea where Odysseus wandered for a decade, the jumbo jets hurtle within the hour.

And far higher than the jets, orbiting astronauts span the distance between ancient Troy and Ithaca in much less than a minute.

Psychologically as well as physically, there are no longer any remote places on earth.

When a friend leaves for what was once a far country, even with no intention of returning, we can't feel that same sense of irrevocable separation that saddened our forefathers.

We know that we are only hours apart by jet, and that we have merely to touch a keyboard to hear a familiar voice.

Or better still, we can now see a beloved face with our modern technology.

The world can shrink no more on us. It has already become a dimensionless point.

But the new stage that is opening up for the human drama will never shrink as the old one has done.

We have abolished space here on this little earth of ours.

We can't however, abolish the space that yawns between the stars.

Once again as in the long-ago days of Troy when Homer sang, we are face to face with immensity, and must accept its grandeur and terror, its inspiring possibilities and its dreadful restraints.

From a world that has become much too small for us, we are moving out into one that will be far too large.

It will be one whose frontiers will recede away from us, and always will move more swiftly away than we can reach out to them.

Consider first, the fairly modest solar system distances which we are now beginning to challenge.

Though the moon is only a few days away, our space probes take months to reach mars and Venus.

It takes many years to reach the outer planets.

However, when we have harnessed nuclear or alternative energy for space flight, the empire of our sun, will seem to contract until it will become little larger to us than the earth is to us today.

The farthest of the planets will be no more than a week away, and Mars and Venus, only a few hours.

This achievement which I believe will be within a century, might appear to make even the solar system, a comfortable, homely place with such giant planets as Saturn and Jupiter playing much the same role in our thoughts as Africa or Asia does in today's world.

The difference of climate, atmosphere and gravity, fundamental through they are, do not concern us at this moment.

To some extent, this may be true, yet as soon as we pass beyond the orbit of the moon, a mere quarter million miles away, we will meet the first barriers that will separate earth from their scattered children.

***

HISTORY LESSON
(AND AN INTRODUCTION TO THE STORY)

Nearly a hundred thousand million stars are turning in the circle of the milky way.

Long ago other races on the worlds of other suns, must have observed and overcome the problems that we now have as we seek to leave behind us, our planet on the way to outer space.

Think of such civilizations as far back in the fabric of time itself.

Think of their fading afterglow of creation. They would be masters of a universe so young that life as yet, had come only to a handful of worlds.

Theirs would have been a loneliness we cannot imagine.

The loneliness of gods, looking out across infinity and finding none to share their thoughts and lives with.

They must have searched the star clusters as we ourselves have searched our solar system for other life.

Everywhere there would be worlds, but they would be empty or peopled with crawling, mindless things.

Such was our own earth in its early days with the smoke of the great volcanoes still staining the skies.

IMPORTANT DISCLAIMER BY BUD

Please allow me to refer you way back to the first part of the book in the section titled "Former Ghost Writer Tells It All."

This is where I touched upon all the many years that I performed services as a ghost writer.

Ghost writing was a profession that I was very good at for over fifty years, and one that I have put behind me so as to allow myself the time needed to become a writer of novels, such as this one.

Everything that has been written up to the prologue and story of proceeding this disclaimer is my own with exception of course of the quoted material, articles, and speeches referenced, and is based upon my personal experiences with meetings, personalities, and minor adventures on my part.

There is no chance of a conflict up to this point.

However, in the pages to come, from to the end of the following storyline, there is a slight possibility of a conflict of wording is possible.

All of what I am using as story material from this point on *is* my own personal creation. However, please keep in mind that I have consulted with many writers over the years, and have offered them many suggestions, written words, and thoughts that might be similar to what I am using here. Because after all it was me writing and conceiving them.

I truly do not know if one single word of what I helped others put together for their works has ever been published or merely thrown out of the stories they were working on. I don't know if my turning of a phrase or idea ever got to print in some other name, but it could have and quite possibly did.

Just in case my words *are* out there, having been used by another, I wish to put this disclaimer into effect.

If anyone wishes to purchase the content of this complete novel, it may only be done with the understanding that from this page on, only a screen play can make use of the ideas and wordings expressed by myself.

A screen play will use different ways of expressing these written words, and often are changed and revised several times over, and I will professionally feel better as I will avoid a conflict with people that I have learned to love over the years.

My deepest respect,
Bud Seligson

And now, at long last, we begin the storyline based upon all of the preceding information that you have absorbed up to now.

PROLOGUE

The ship was alone.

She was moving, and moving fast, but there was nothing around her to show how fast she was going.

She seemed to be suspended within a featureless universe of gray, transfixed in an empty fog, beyond space, beyond time, beyond understanding.

There were no stars, no planets, and no far galaxies that glowed like milky jewels against the shadowed velvet of space.

There was just the ship, and the complete grayness and that was all.

The high irritating hum of the atomics powering the warp drive filled the ship.

The warp drive was a faster-than-light propulsion system that could travel at speeds greater than that of the speed of light.

The warp drive was called "a gravimetric field displacement manifold," and it was being powered by a mater/antimatter reaction coil, which created a displacement field around the entire ship.

This allowed the ship to move within the very folds of hyper-space itself.

In doing so, the ship could travel great distances within a small-time frame.

Aboard the ship, time continued to pass in the usual way for the passengers and crew, while the ship itself hurled forward in what was a slingshot effect that exceeded the speed of light many times over.

Under the warp drive formula, the ship was capable of traveling at a warp factor of 5 which would be about 125 times the speed of light.

The ship and its company of humanoids could go anywhere in their known universe, and get back home again within a reasonable timeline of a few years.

The home that they would be going back to was far behind them in space and time.

This ship was searching, searching a galaxy as other ships had searched before her, and would search after her.

She was searching for hope, and so far, there was none.

Mankind had found many things in space as its fleet of warp-speed vessels fanned out across the universe.

They had found many new worlds and they had found new marvels that amazed them beyond their scientific understanding.

But they had also found loneliness and no hope at all among all the worlds of all the suns that could and did support life.

It would not have been so bad if they had found no evidence of other men just like them.

It would have been perfectly fine if they had just found empty land and empty seas and volcano's bursting out with hot lava everywhere.

But this was not what they had found and the reality of their discovery had quickly become known to them all.

When their warp-field drive had been mastered, making possible interstellar flight in a matter of months instead of generations, the first exploring ships had gone out eagerly and confidently.

Of course, they went out armed to the teeth, ready for the monsters that their myths had prepared them for. But they were also ready to find other humanoids.

They were hoping to find men and women of their own kind, or even different in many ways, but still humanoid.

They were all drilled, trained and disciplined, so that there would be no awkward incidents, and no immediate misunderstanding that might lead to a disaster of some sort between them.

They were after all, looking for friends and not enemies.

They were looking in the starry universe that was their own home, for other men, other intelligence, other civilizations.

The people of their homeworld of Enaid, were not foolish enough to believe that one world, their world, was the only world that held intelligent life.

They began to think of themselves as living on an isolated island, completely cut off from contact with other islands and continents, by the vast sea of space.

They were wise enough to realize that a planet alone would amount to something much less than a planet that was part of something bigger. Something that would bring their culture in contact with other cultures and allow them to all grow together.

Cultures grow through contact with other cultures, because no great civilization that they knew of, grew in one sealed area, with only its own ideas to keep it going.

These cultures and civilizations, without other contacts, were doomed to die. Because without fresh viewpoints, new ideas, different historical traditions, these were the ingredients of a doomed world.

Alone, that planet could go so far and no further.

There is a point in which it exhausts itself, no matter how rich, varied and special that culture may be.

There will always be a time when it comes to a complete stop.

Life is a process. It means change, development, and challenge.

When it merely repeats itself, when it only survives, it becomes at best, insignificant, and sooner or later the effort is too much for it and it becomes extinct.

And there comes a time also, in the history of civilizations, when technology is not enough.

When gadgets no longer satisfy.

There comes a time when science itself can be seen in perspective, a method, a technique, that can't supply all the answers that are needed.

Man is really an advanced animal who asks questions. He asks them constantly, and incessantly.

He asks questions as soon as he can speak, and he continues to ask questions as long as he lives.

When men no longer question things, and when they are complacent enough to believe that they know everything that they need to know, then they are finished, absolutely finished.

They may continue to eat, work, sleep, make love and go through the routine of life, but the truth of the matter is that they are finished as a people.

The people of Enaid were still asking questions, but they were tougher questions than they had asked with Enaid was a younger world.

They knew there were no ultimate, final answers, but they were alive enough to want to keep trying.

It was these questions that sent the men and women of Enaid out to the stars.

Not rare minerals, not national defense, not even science in the strict sense of the word.

It was questions that sent them out there and they were the same old questions but just being asked in a different way.

What lies over yonder?

What lies behind the mountains of space?

Does a sun shine down on humanoid life out there?

Do warm breezes blow as they do on our planet Enaid?

Would our people be happy "there?" And just where is "there?"

And so, the men of Enaid locked their bodies in shining cylinders and flamed and thundered outward into the great unknown.

Not all of them, of course. Most people anywhere, are content with whatever they have, because change is too much trouble.

But many of them went, at first, with a calm efficiency that they could not hide in their eyes.

They were going to find a companion planet somewhere in the universe, so that their planet would not continue on into the ages alone.

They were determined that their planet would survive forever, as soon as they found a soulmate.

They went out and they looked, and when they all came back, the look in their eyes, and the spring in their step was gone.

That was the beginning of the end of the dream of finding other humanoids.

That was the beginning of the horror that waited for them "out there."

***

They did find other men.

Other men who were just like themselves.

But instead of the beginning of their great and wonderful dream, everything turned into a nightmare.

They brought back evidence of other humanoid civilizations, just like they had on their own home planet.

With the passing of time, all the ships that had gone out with such great and grand hopes, came back sad and disappointed with the results of all their efforts.

There must be some mistake, they all said. They can't be men like we are men.

But the anatomists said: "they are men." The biologists said: "they are men."

There were many differences from world to world, but the differences were for the most part not important.

There were variations in blood type, in body temperature, in skin color, in the number of vertebrae.

Man, was not a rare animal in the universe after all, and it was the very height of egotism to imagine that he was.

All isolated peoples believe that they are the only human being in the world, and when a planet thinks itself to be alone, before the ships go out into space, it is difficult for the people on that planet to conceive of other human beings elsewhere among the stars.

Why, man evolved here, they told each other on a million worlds, nodding wisely at their own wisdom.

He is amazingly complex, and the line that led to him was a long shot, an accident and that could never happen again.

And they thought it, even if they did not say it out loud, that we are wonderful, we can be found only here on this wonderful world of ours.

Our planet that we all live on, has been singled out by creation as the one, the only, and the original home of great big adorable us.

Some knew this to be true: others fiddled with statistics.

They all ignored the supreme fact. They were taking a sample of one, their own speck of dust, and generalizing from it to the entire universe.

Moreover, they were generalizing in a silly way, for the one planet they had in their sample had evolved human life, and that made it unanimous, as far as they actually knew.

It was not that man was foreordained, built in from the beginning.

It was simply that the evolution of intelligence, of the ability to develop culturally, necessarily proceeded along the road of trial and error, change and modification.

A culture-bearing animal had to be warm blooded, for he needed the energy. He had to be big brained, and he had to have free hands and specialized feet.

A manlike form was the mechanical answer to one trend of evolution, and if conditions permitted, he came along sooner or later.

And so, based upon the above logic, there were other men similar to the men on the home planet of Enaid.

But the question that needed to be asked was "what had happened to these other men on these other planets?"

The reports came in, brought home by ships across the light years.

For a short time, a very short time, there seemed to be little consistency to ·these reports.

Then the pattern began to emerge and was only repeated, as the number of reports grew to a hundred, to five hundred, to a thousand.

And just what was that pattern?

Well, stripped of its technical language, it boiled down to something elementary, something frightful in its simplicity.

The ships had discovered three kinds of planets that had developed mankind.

On one type, the men had not yet advanced to a state of technological development that gave them a chance to destroy themselves.

On a second type, above the primitive level, but not yet to the level of space flight, men were organized into groups, busily hacking away at each other with whatever weapons they could put together.

On these worlds, our visitors from the planet Enaid, were received with suspicion, with hostility, with fear.

Their ships were impounded and their knowledge was used to fight in wars that were utterly meaningless to them.

Crews that landed on these worlds seldom if ever got home again.

And there was a third type, where man had evolved quite far.

They had developed weapons. Powerful enough to do the job, and man made himself extinct.

The methods varied: germs, crop blights, cobalt bombs, gas and so on.

The results were the same on all of these planets. The results were extinction.

In all the universe that they could reach, this was what had become of man. As soon as he was able to do it, he destroyed himself.

Ho, friend and neighbor.

Many thanks for the inspiring example you have set for us.

And us, what of us? Are we not men, the same as they were?

This, indeed was the catch.

The civilization of Enaid was an old civilization, and thought of itself as being sophisticated.

It had weathered many a storm and it had survived.

The people had always felt a certain pride in this, and suddenly they had evidence to show them how right, or how foolish, this pride was.

For Enaid, alone of all the worlds in the known universe, had spawned mankind, watched him develop a mighty technology, and lived to tell the tale.

At first, even for a sophisticated people, this was a boost for the ego.

They, and they alone, had mastered the art of living with each other in peace, and even in friendship.

We're different.

We've succeeded.

We're better than "they" are, smarter, and wiser.

There was a religious revival, a time of thanksgiving and the inevitable cults appeared along with the inexorable political philosophies.

They said we should pull in our explorers, stay at home, live our own lives.

Let us rejoice in our own goodness, keep away from other men, and cultivate our own garden.

Why, others asked?

Because we are different, unique and much better.

Aren't we?

Aren't we?

This initial unthinking smugness could not last. It was a frail balloon at best, easily punctured by factual needles.

And the facts were not pleasant. When all due allowances were made, when logic had been twisted until it could bend no more, the truth behind all of this was still there.

Out of a thousand and more worlds of men, all had perished as soon as they were capable of it.

There were no exceptions.

Men were the same everywhere, the same in the things that counted.

The men of Enaid were not different.

They had survived for three hundred years after they had learned to control their first atomic reactor.

They had patched up their differences and there had been no wars.

They knew that wars were obsolete when the first atomic bomb became possible, and they knew that wars, ultimately meant suicide.

But other people had known it too.

The books taken from shattered libraries on lifeless planets were full of it.

They had known and they were gone.

Question: Is three hundred years long enough to let us relax?

Question: Is man of necessity self-destructive?

Question: If we go on living alone, never find another civilization to build the future with, what will become of us?

These questions were too tough for individual minds, but they were not too tough for computers.

The data was fed in, the questions asked, and the answers given.

Other peoples had lasted three hundred years after harnessing the atom, but they had gone under eventually.

The computer said that the odds were that man would always destroy himself.

There was a chance, the computers said, that this was not true, but it was a very slim one.

If Enaid built a figurative wall around itself, buried its head in the sand, its civilization would endure for a long time.

It had gained that much by living past its first great crisis period.

It might go on for thirty thousand years more, but it would gradually begin to slow down and finally it would lose all of its vitality and stop.

One day it would be all gone.

What could they do?

The analysis of the data showed one possibility.

No human culture on record had ever succeeded in finding and establishing friendly relations with another human culture on a different planet.

If a world could be found where men were sane, if contacts could be build up between them, if ideas and hopes and dreams could flow from one to the other, then all things would be possible.

Then perhaps man might someday be more than just another animal who lost his way.

He might just be more than another extinct animal who couldn't change when the times changed around him.

Then perhaps man could play a fuller role in the ebb and flow that was life in the universe.

If only a world could be found.

The ships kept going out. But they had to go farther now, into parts of the galaxy so remote that the suns were no more than numbers in the great catalogues of the stars.

They had to go farther, and still they found nothing, and worse than nothing.

The world they needed was well hidden, if indeed it existed at all.

But the ships kept flaming outward, but their numbers dwindled as they had trouble finding crew members who still believed.

A ship had to stay out for over seven years in order to cover any area at all, and who wanted to go into space for seven years?

CHAPTER ONE

The ship was alone...

The high irritating hum of the atomics powering the warp drive still filled the ship as an inner door slid open and Wyat, the tall and extremely good looking navigator stepped into the large cabin.

He was erect and outwardly calm, as his strange black eyes swept over the others sitting around the room with concern.

"Captain Jenka has asked me to advise you all to strap yourselves in."

"Is the displacement field still acting up?" Alexa, the only female on board asked with a touch of concern in her very soft voice.

"Some, Yes."

Navigator Wyat could not help looking directly at Alexa as she asked her question.

She was easy to look at, and he took a moment to let his eyes take their time as they roamed over her body.

She was tall, athletic looking, and absolutely drop-dead gorgeous.

She was a reporter who was on board to write about life aboard a starship explorer, and she always had a smile on her most pleasing of faces.

Wyat liked the way her high cheekbones and her sparkling eyes lit up when she talked to him.

She was wearing a civilian outfit that was quite different from the plain looking astronaut suits that the rest of the crew wore as standard aboard-ship uniforms.

Her leisure suit was cut just right to give a hint of her magnificent bosom that peeked out at him ever so slightly.

She was sitting at her writing desk with her legs crossed to show off a great deal of thigh, as she leaned back in her cushioned writing chair.

She postured herself so that she could arch her back and point her breasts at Wyatt as she spoke to him.

This limited view of her breasts brought back to his mind the wonderful night a week ago, when Alexa had tiptoed into his cabin.

He was awakened by the rustle of the covers as a well perfumed slender body slid itself next to him.

She was wearing only a thin shift and Wyat who was wearing rather less, was keenly aware of the warm, female body that was pressed against his own bare flesh.

She molded herself up against him and without speaking a word between them, he ran his hands in a brief caress.

He determined that her shoulders were straight, her breasts were full and high, and her hips slender but most generously curved.

What more could one ask of so willing a female?

Her mouth opened to receive the heated branding of his searching tongue.

A soft moan escaped her lips as she felt a simmering heat in the very depths of her being. She had been wondering what kind of a lover the Navigator would make and she was about to find out.

Being the only woman aboard ship gave her many opportunities to try out each of the male crew members as potential bed partners.

So far, she had worked her way through four of the eight men aboard. She eliminated the Captain from her mental checklist and calculated that after tonight there were only two more guys to check out.

She loved her job and all the strange and exotic places it sent her.

Navigator Wyat's ears were filled with the soft sounds coming from deep within Alexa's throat, as he held her crushed against him.

As his lips left her mouth, he tasted the softness of her cheek, the fragile curve of her jaw and the slim line of her throat.

As he placed moist kisses along the upper edge of her shoulders, he felt the straining fullness of her breasts.

There was still not a word spoken between them as he lowered his lips and placed feathery kisses between the valley created by her breasts, while his fingers brushed against the hardened tips.

The girl inhaled sharply as she felt the soft caress of his fingers going down her spine.

But she released her held breath just as quickly, as his head lowered once again down to her breasts.

Sheer carnal desire flamed throughout her body, as his lips settled over one rose-colored nipple.

As he suckled the tender tip, her limbs weakened and she felt a bit out of her usual control.

His mouth consumed hers once more with its searching demand, as his tongue pushed forward and finding no resistance from the compliant female, he sought out and touched each and every curve of her body, as he once again began tracing a very tempting path down to her ever-waiting breast.

As he drew a sweet nipple into his mouth, her body trembled with a deep, wanton desire that left her clutching at his head as she pressed herself more firmly against him.

In the soft nightlights that lit up the room with a pleasant glow, Wyat stared down at the wonderful curves of perfection that he could see lying there waiting on his pleasure.

The heated flames within his eyes seared every inch of her flesh, as he gazed upon the fullness of her twin globes, with their dusty rose-colored buds.

His eyes roamed down the length of her trim rib cage, down to the tiny indent of her navel, and across the womanly flare of her hips, and finally down the long and shapely legs.

Wyat, at age twenty-six, had bedded down a fair share of girls so far in his lifetime.

Most of them were local girls from other branches of the air services that were scattered around his home base.

There were also a few native city girls who he knew when he would get time off from the job and could head into the city with some of his fellow astronauts.

BUT, he thought quickly, as he was really quite busy with the young lady who occupied his full attention at that moment, that female reporters were absolutely everything "they" said about them and more.

CHAPTER TWO

Wyat's gaze caressed the delicate ankles and slim feet of the beautiful reporter.

He drew himself halfway up, eyes filling with burning desire as he looked down upon the junction of her womanhood, with the feathering of dark, curling hair lending a definite contrast to the creamy, pearl iridescence of her skin.

As his eyes returned to her face, she was parting her lips as if to speak, but upon her seeing the desire in his eyes, she was content to know the power her woman's body now was having over this man.

At that moment, she knew that the Navigator desired her above anything else in his life.

This indeed was raw, female power, and her own passion-laced desires welcomed his seduction.

The irresistible pull of pleasure's promise, grabbed her body as Wyat's mouth again roamed over her.

Feathered kisses, licking and nibbling, he ravished her breast once again. His straight white teeth caressing the under-flesh of her breasts, were beginning to drive her mad with her own heated desire.

A soft moan escaped from deep within her throat, and at the same time, his dark head lowered to her ribs, and the tempting curves of her waist and hips.

The taste of her sweet flesh, and the feel of her satin-smooth body, combined to seduce Wyat into a physical wanting that knew no bounds.

His hands splayed over the firmness of her belly, and then pressed on closer to her hips.

His tongue sent flames shooting throughout the lower portion of her body, as he rubbed the inside of her thighs.

As his mouth touched her woman's jewel, she bucked as sweet, forbidden pleasure snaked through her womb and thrashing limbs.

Without mercy, Wyat kept up his love play, his tongue plunging into her moist, sweet depths, and lingering over the extremely sensitive nub, as she shuddered again and again.

Her soft cries filled his ears and fueled his desire to pleasure her to the fullest.

As the trembling of her body slowly subsided, and the fingers within his hair lessened their tight hold, Wyat rose from his position between her thighs.

His lips seared branding kisses over her body, as he finally pressed his length of manhood against her.

His eyes witnessed the sated passion on her face before he covered her mouth once more with his own.

The girl gave herself completely up to him, being too swept up in the steaming rapture of the moment to do otherwise.

As Wyat's tongue filled her mouth, she felt the sculptured, marble-head of his "love-tool" pressing at the opening between her parted legs.

Her buttocks drew upward, and as he entered her, just an inch or so, she felt the tightness of her own passage.

Another thrust and another inch as he felt the velvet trembling of her inner sanctum yield before his entry.

A low rumbling came from within his own chest and filled the entire room with his animal like noises.

He moved back and forth and in and out, going slowly deeper

and deeper, and then he would withdraw back to the "Very lips of her moist opening.

Over and over he plied her with his skillful seduction, until she was clutching his back, with her head thrown back wildly, as the fullness in her loins drove her toward a frenzy of mindless desire.

Each time the brand of his lance drove into her depths and stirred her, her body moved closer toward its completion.

Her legs slowly rose and fell as she sought to capture and hold onto the entire length of him that was now deeply inside her.

Still holding himself back somewhat, Wyat caught hold of her buttocks, and with a talent born of past lovemaking, he maintained his inner control.

Even as he felt the shuddering coming from the lady beneath him, he was able to inhale a few deep breaths of air, willing himself not to release the final fury of his passion.

Wyat knew the power of her climax, and for a moment or two, he fought his own heated need that was racing through his own loins.

He watched her passion-filled face and heard the climatic moans escaping from her throat.

Each thrust was now torture-laced for him, as he fought off the aching need for his own fulfillment.

Only when he felt her climax receding, did he allow himself to give full vent to his own desire.

His mouth covered hers, and as he plunged just a fraction deeper into her soft velvety depths, wildfire absolutely caught up within him.

Scalding pleasure burst forth from the very center of his being, and showered upward, racing through his most powerful lance.

It took Wyat several minutes to regain his normal breathing, and to conquer the disbelief that filled his brain.

He knew that he would remember these moments for the rest of his life, and he just relaxed with it and let things slowly come to an end with this exciting woman.

A huge shudder coursed its way through him, as he realized that he had personally never been driven to such powerful feeling of lust before.

He felt himself wondering if she had felt the same feelings, or if this was just another interesting bed time adventure for her to have aboard ship.

Turning his face so that he could gaze into her eyes, he found her eyelids closed, her breathing soft, and her arms caressing his neck.

She slept peacefully in his arms, and a small smile filtered over his lips.

Not that it mattered, but he didn't know anything about her except that she was a reporter. And that also did not matter to him.

Tomorrow would be time enough for the two of them to talk.

For now, he just wanted to enjoy the moment.

Sleep, slow and pleasant came to him in the most wonderful manner.

All was quiet within the darkened room.

CHAPTER THREE

Navigator Wyat forced his attention away from looking at reporter Alexa, and continued to look at everyone sitting around the community room.

Tenya, the Geologist, whose job was to deal with the geological time and physical nature of a planet's inner and outer core, was in the control room with the Captain, and had already heard the instructions that Wyat was told to bring to the rest of the nine-person crew.

Golan, the Archeologist, was sitting next to Alexa, and they were playing some sort of a card game.

Golan made the official reports on the life and the culture of past, ancient civilizations. This was done by excavation of ancient cities, relics, artifacts, etc.

For the past three years of countless landings, they had found lots of evidence that humanoids had once lived on the surfaces of the planets, but no living beings were ever located.

It was almost the same story everytime they stopped. It was evident that mankind of one type or another had lived there, but no sign of life was evident due to atomic wars of one type or other.

Wyat was wondering to himself about how does one describe the sadness that they were finding everywhere they went.

How does one describe the sadness of centuries?

What epitaph do you inscribe on the tombstone of man?

What lines would they scribble in their notebook, what could they find to tell what they were seeing here and there, on a world that was less than a name back home.

All those words had been already used by the hundreds of ships and crews who had done the same thing they were now doing, and getting the same terrible results.

Whenever they had walked the streets of one civilized empty planet or other, they all thought about other men, native to this planet who had walked down these very same streets.

No sand then, no jagged concrete ruptures, no decay and collapse and fire scars.

Trees, perhaps, green grass. A buzz of commerce, a blur of faces, some happy, some sad, some handsome, some ugly.

A news screen with words and pictures from around the world. What had been news to them, so near the end?

What could they have been thinking about, talking about, joking about:

"THE WEATHER TOMORROW WILL BE FAIR AND CLOUDY, WITH LIGHT RAIN IN THE AFTERNOON.

THE GREENS WON THE SILVER TROPHY TODAY ON A SENSATIONAL PLAY BY....

THE SITUATION IN OCEANIA APPEARS TO BE MORE SERIOUS THAN EVERYONE FIRST THOUGHT, BUT THE COUNCIL SAYS THERE IS NO CAUSE FOR ALARM."

ETC. ETC. ETC.

And the libraries. Wyat's favorite place wherever they landed, was always the libraries.

He would climb inside the broken-down walls and scramble inside with his flashlight beam sending little tunnels of pale light into the gloom.

His footsteps would echo down silent corridors. Sand would be everywhere, and dust rose before him in puffs and clouds.

He always looked for periodicals and history books and picked up tapes at random.

He would always take a novel or two. In the back of his mind he would be thinking that the author probably thought that his stuff would live forever. No chance for that now.

What should one take from a library that belonged to the city of the dead? What words should you select for the linguists back home to analyze, or for the computers to buzz over, or for the newspapers to sensationalize.

What lines could you find that would add up to one more footnote in one more history of man?

They already had maps of each city, photographed from the ship, so they all spent most of their remaining time inside the ruins of houses, preserving what little they could on film.

When they were all though, they returned as they had come, back through the littered streets, out again into the sand sculptures of the yellow desert.

The wind would moan in their faces, blowing into the city, whining around jagged buildings and through black holes that had once been windows.

Into the ships airlock quickly, for the cold and empty night was falling.

The outside port hissed shut. The dry air of the planet was pumped out, given back to a world that no longer needed it.

Then the inner port opened, and they were safely back in the ship.

Shake the sand from your boots, wash the sand from your body.

Put on clean clothes, clothes that do not smell of the dust and decay and the centuries of emptiness.

"That does it," they would say. "Another world shot to hell."

It was always difficult, and always hard not to remember the emptiness.

It was always difficult after a field party came back.

What were the odds now, the odds against their own planet's survival?

A million to one?

A billion to one?

Try not to think about it. Do your job. Cry if you must.

Laugh it off if you can.

Mankind seemed doomed.

Doomed.

Wyat was taken out of his personal trip down the sentimental journey that had his thoughts all tied up by Bald, who was the leader of the three-man maintenance crew who were responsible for carrying out the captain's orders, maintenance of just about everything that moved on board the vessel, and were the go-to-guys for just about anything.

The work crew consisted of himself, and the brothers Volpa and Lopa who followed his orders.

Bakl, the crew chief, was saying to Wyat, in his booming voice that carried easily throughout the room, "was there something the Captain wanted you to tell us, Wyat?"

"I don't wish to alarm any of you, but we can't conceal a problem that has come up in engineering."

He looked at each of them in turn. "We had trouble coming out of the last distortion field and the Captain feels that we may have trouble again."

"He has made a decision to spend some additional time on the next planet that we come to and make the necessary repairs, and then get ourselves home."

"It is his thought that this next stopover will be our last, and while those of us who go out into this world to do our scientific investigation, he and the maintenance crew will fix the problem and then set our course for home."

He asked me to tell you that even though this will mean cutting our exploration time by over a year, our safety and the safety of the ship comes first."

"Is there anyone who might have a question about what I have just said?"

Paill, the historian asked, "since this will be the last stopover, please ask the Captain if there is anything different he wants me to do when we go out for the last time? Are there any artifacts he wants us to gather? Kindly ask him if this is just another routine examination of the planet, or are we doing something special at our last stop?"

"I'll surely find out for you Paill. As soon as things calm down in the command room, I'll get you an answer."

"I'm going forward to assist the Captain, is there anything anyone else would like me to find out?"

All heads shook no, and Wyat took his leave. He was thinking that the question that the Historian raised was a good one. If this was going to be our last landing before going home, was there something different that needed to be done.

It was Paill, the Historian who, after all was said and done, and all the reports were compiled and sent in to command headquarters, would put together the complete copy of what they saw, what they did, and what conclusions each different department head had to add.

Hoping that he had calmed any fears that the members of the expedition might have had, he took his leave and headed to the forward command post to report to the Captain that everyone was agreeable to his thoughts about the repairs and then getting underway for home.

CHAPTER FOUR

Three months had now passed since Wyat had told them about the last stop that they were going to make before the long journey home.

Alexa was a very detailed young lady.

Every evening after she had dinner with whoever was in the community room, she would retire to her corner where she kept her computer and all her paperwork in a small filling cabinet.

Even if nothing was happening and the hours dragged on as the ship hurtled itself through space, she would make a brief summary of the day's happenings, even if they were "boring as hell."

She wanted to be able to go back to her daily notes that would recall every single detail to mind when she finally got back home and began to write her story.

She was excited about what she was going to write. She thought that she would write it as a first-person narrative, which meant that she would write about things exactly as she experienced them.

The only thing that was not entered into her secret-coded computer was about her personal life aboard ship.

Who she slept with and how good they were in bed was not anyone else's business.

More than likely, she would have all of her tremendous amounts of notes transcribed, and then rewritten by her magazine's professional writers.

She expected to make so much money from her aboard ship stories that she could retire into a life of luxury.

She often thought about what she wanted to do when she had nothing but time and money, but she put off thinking about that for another day.

Alexa knew that she was a very healthy and normal girl, and having sex every once in a while, was as much of her life as eating and sleeping.

It did not hurt her at all, knowing that every man on board, except the Captain, who maintained his distance from everyone, looked at her with longing.

After all, they were without women in their lives for years and years, and watching her walk around was the only sexual fantasy available to them.

She decided that she would make herself available to each of them except for the Captain and the two workers, Volpa and Lopa. She felt that they were beneath her station in life.

There was only one person left on her list to be visited, and that was Bald the chief engineer. She wondered how he would be in the sack.

He had that barrel chest and arms that were swelled with muscles. She thought about him each night, just as she was falling asleep.

She thought that making love with him would be an interesting experience. She was aware of his looking at her just like all the other men did.

And thinking about all the other men, it was Wyat, the Navigator who was the best lover of all. After she had finally experienced Bakl in her bed, it probably would be Wyat that she would spend the rest of the nights with as they winged their way home after the repairs.

But for the moment, Bakl was the next on her list. It was absolutely wonderful being the only female on board the space ship. Life was fabulous and she was having the time of her life.

Going back early from the seven-year voyage that she had

signed up for, was a wonderful thing. She already had more than enough stuff in her computer to write all the stories that would be demanded from her.

The extra years off of the voyage would be hers to enjoy.

She could see herself on the lecture tour, writing books and being the name on everyone's lips back home.

Life was good and she was enjoying every single moment of it.

She planned on seeing Bakl later that evening when everything quieted down after dinner.

She would wait until everyone said goodnight to each other, and then she would sneak into his room.

Alexa also wondered if everyone knew what she was doing with her visitations?

Almost everyone had one of her visits and she assumed that they all knew that she was making the rounds.

She was looking forward to much later that night when she would be visiting Bakl.

He should be quite the interesting stud.

***

The only light in the room was coming from a small floor lamp that stood in the comer as Bakl put his arms around the beautiful girl who had slipped into his unlocked compartment door.

The feel of his rough hands running over her naked back as he held her close, seemed so right.

It felt good to her, to have him holding her as he felt the heat of his large body coming through to her.

Suddenly they were deeply kissing each other, drinking in each other with a deep intensity.

Alexa felt the usual feeling she would get during sex, that if she didn't have him right away, she would absolutely die.

Her tongue stoked his in return.

He twined his fingers into her hair, tugging away the leather band that was holding it at the nape of her neck.

She leaned firmly into him and felt the thick ridge of his large erection.

Bakl quickly filled his hands with her high, full breasts and stroked her plump pink nipples.

He lifted her up as if she was a child and carried her carefully over to the waiting bed where he deposited her face down.

He carefully positioned her so that she was on her hands and knees. This was a new position for her and one that she had heard about from some of her girlfriends but had not experienced herself yet.

He showed her how to put her weight on her forward leaning hands which gave the rest of her supple body more freedom of movement.

She immediately caught the idea, and lifted up her rear end higher, with her legs nicely spread out.

Bahl was very pleased that there was no need to talk to this compliant woman.

He reached forward and played with her beautiful breasts for a few minutes. She really had a great set of breasts.

He slowly entered her from the rear, and carefully began to pump into her with a slow but ever increasing motion.

This was something new for Alexa and the sensations that she was getting from his entry were new and completely different from what she was used to. It was wonderful and she began to enjoy herself tremendously and with much enthusiasm.

She caught onto the rocking motion quickly, and very shortly the two of them were moving back and forth with a steady and ever increasing motion.

It wasn't long before the two of them were pumping away together for all that they were worth.

Minutes later, Bakl was done and Alexa, with a loud scream

completed her own sexual fulfillment.

Very soon, the two of them were fast asleep with Bakl's head lying gently between her breasts....

CHAPTER FIVE

Several weeks have now passed, and the ship was entering the general star system where they were planning to make their last stop, and do the repairs before the long *trip* back home to Enaid.

The topic of conversation among the crew was telling their favorite stories about home.

It was a cheerful time, and everyone seemed to be in a good place, as they filled in their down time with conversations, computer games and laughter.

Things were quite different in the control room where the Captain and Wyat the Navigator were at their posts moving with a calmness that could not hide the tension they were both feeling.

Their faces were curiously pale in the white light as Wyat was slowly moving from control panel to control panel and calling out a series of figures that the Captain was entering into the ship's main computer system.

The Navigator's tall, slender body seemed strained as he sighed with relief as his panels told them that they would have no problem getting to the yellow sun that it saw in the distance.

The Captain hovered over Wyat's shoulder, as they both watched the data coming out of the panel control unit.

"Well," the Captain was saying, "How much time have we got until the atomics start acting up again?"

"Maybe twenty-four hours," Wyat said carefully.

"Maybe less. It is hard to tell right now. This has never happened before."

"I suggest Captain, that we set our course directly toward the third planet that we previously talked about."

"This was the one that the computer told us had some signs of life on the surface areas."

"I agree with the computer that it is our best location for our layover."

"Wyat, think your answer out carefully before you give it to me. Are the atomic motors as bad as I think they are, and if the answer is affirmative, do you believe that we can make it to that third planet before they fail?"

"Captain, there is really nothing for me to think about. We should have no problem getting to that planet, and we may even be able to circle around it a few times to get a feel for what it is like."

"What I'm not comfortable with, is when we are ready to settle down and land somewhere."

"The motors in the reverse landing position seem to be breaking down right now and could cause us problems."

"This means that we will either land smoothly without a problem, or we will land in an emergency situation where we could be in real trouble."

"There is no way of knowing in advance. The computers tell us everything is fine, but some of the reading are a bit off scale, and that worries me. I don't like to be worried, and I think we should be prepared for the worse situation possible."

"We are definitely too far away from home to turn around without properly working atomics. We could never get into the distortion field without them."

"As we have agreed, we need to land and make repairs, and if those repairs fail, then that planet that is orbiting that sun, will be our new home for a long time, until the distress signal that we will send out gets home, and they send someone out to get us."

"I know this sounds very negative, but this is my honest opinion and I strongly suggest you bring the rest of the company into this conversation."

"It is best if you tell them the entire truth and lay it all on the line.

"They are all professionals, and they should be able to handle whatever happens next."

The captain nodded at Wyat and walked over to the small writing desk that he kept in the far corner of the control room.

He composed himself and began to write down the various points that he wished to make when he spoke to the crew.

He had thought about having a face to face meeting with everyone right now, but he thought it best not to have one.

There would be too many questions, and too many personalities involved for a face to face. He would have Wyat hook up the sound system so that his voice could be heard throughout the entire ship.

He read over his notes and then told Wyat to do the connection so that everyone would hear him at the same time.

It was about fifteen minutes later until Wyat told him that everything was ready for him.

***

The usual three chimes rang, followed by a ten second pause, and then the captain came on the air with his usual crisp and clear way of speaking.

"Good afternoon everyone.

"This is the captain speaking to you from the control room, where I am now working with navigator Wyat.

"It seems very possible that the atomic motors might be causing us a problem that will concern us all.

"We won't know if we really have a problem until we make a

landing on the third planet circling the small yellow star that we are heading for right now.

"Our first computer readout tells us the planet will be friendly to us with proper gravity, enough land mass, and a perfect reading of the gases in the atmosphere so that we can breathe the air without any problems.

"As I look out the window screen that shows our surroundings, I'm seeing the black sea of normal space, which means we have completely gotten out of the distortion field, and I can see the friendly points of lights of stars in the distance.

"I suggest that you all go to the nearest outside window-screen and see the comforting sight of normal space that is surrounding us."

The strange sounding hum of the atomic motors behind the captain's voice did nothing to calm the nerves of the attentive listeners.

The captain continued, "I believe that you can all hear the background whine of the atomics. They actually sound worse than they are.

"We will have no problem getting to that planet and we will be able to circle it a few times to get a complete readout on a landing site.

"We should be able to pick out a good landing location to do our repairs and spend the weeks it will take to fix everything that needs fixing.

"If everything goes well, we will take off immediately, enter the distortion field and head straight for home.

"That would seem to be the best thing to do under those circumstances.

"The worst is that we have a problem landing and if this is true, we probably will damage the ship beyond our ability to repair it.

"Unless the civilization on the planet is advanced enough to be of help to us, we will have to send out a distress signal home, and ask for someone to come and get us.

"The thing about sending out the distress message is that it will give our coordinates with no problem, but it will go out with only the speed of light, and that will take years and years of travel time to get the signal home.

"So, if we have trouble landing, then we had better plan on living out most of our lifetime on the surface of the planet and away from the ship which will not be in any condition to support us.

"I am only painting a worse case situation here so that anything less will seem better.

"Navigator Wyat and I are not optimistic at this time.

"Here are my final orders and I expect them to be followed to the letter. Any and all medications that are needed must be packed in the field back pack, and must be worn by all member of the crew when we are a day away from landing.

"On that last day, all small weapons must be worn by everyone. That means small rifles, pistols and knives.

"Extra bullets, bandages, hand held computers, and so forth must also be included.

"The crew chief will give each person emergency food rations that will go into each back pack, and the chief will be responsible with the inspection of each back pack on the day before we arrive.

"The order of leadership if we are grounded will be the same as it is aboard ship.

"Captain, followed by navigator and then followed by crew chief.

"If we all remain calm and professional, we can come through this with few if any problems.

"The emergency rescue signal is being sent out shortly. If we don't need to be rescued, we will beat the signal home by many years and we will cancel it.

"If we don't cancel it, then one day another ship will come to our location and rescue us.

"My final thought is for after we land or possibly crash land.

"We will be going into a strange world, but it will be familiar to us in that it will support human life.

"The plants and animals will be no problem but the humans might.

"Probably the humans have all killed themselves off, but if they haven't yet, we must be careful not to give advanced information to a civilization that can use what we have to attack our home world.

"The other side of the coin on this, is that the humans might not be very advanced and to them we might seem to be gods.

"If we have to live among primitives, being seen as gods, is not a bad thing. The key to this situation is for our entire crew to stay together as long as possible.

"I can't think of anything else at the moment but everything is open to discussion.

"We are planning on having group meetings. As soon as possible to prepare for the worst-case situation.

"Captain out."

CHAPTER SIX

The ship moved on, swimming through the star-flecked seas of space.

A flaming yellow sun floated ahead of her, with scarlet gas prominences puffing out from its equator and then raining back into the photosphere.

The ship was a tiny thing, lost in the immensity of the universe.

It was a speck of dust, and less than that.

And yet it was not insignificant, even here.

If the flare of the ship's atomics was only a dot of light against the furnace of the sun, she still carried life and hope and fear.

The silent challenge she threw at the abyss of not-life, around her was a comic thing, and yet in its way, it outshone the splendor of the stars.

The days passed.

The ship picked her way toward the third planet, intersecting its orbit as it swung about its sun.

Outwardly, the ship showed no sign that it was in trouble as it moved gracefully and serenely as a canoe does in quiet waters.

Inside the ship, it was quite different.

The third planet hung hugely in the view-screen, a globe of blue and green that blotted out the stars.

White clouds banded the world, looking astonishingly like breakers in a choppy sea.

There was a glint at the poles that hinted of ice, and lots of it.

The ship screamed down into the atmosphere and the noise inside the control room turned into a bedlam of sound.

The atomics gave out their piercing sounds, and the computers chattered as the very metal of the ship itself groaned in protest.

"Four miles," called the Navigator. "We'll cut across the equator, and then circle the poles. That way we can get the best pictures of all the landscape."

The planet flashed by under them, a mosaic of continents and clouds and sea.

The Captain stared at the control panels and found that he was holding his breath. He let it out slowly and forced himself to breathe normally.

The Captain made a decision. "We're still too high up for a good view of the land. If we are going to decide where the best place to land will be, we need to get lower. See what you can do, Navigator."

Navigator Wyat was grinning. "Hang on he said as he reset the course to just skim above some of the higher mountain peaks.

"I'll get you a closer look at everything I can, Captain. Just give me a few minutes to make all the adjustments."

The ship roared and slashed her way down, blasting through the high clouds with her hot metal sides hissing.

She straightened out over the land masses, jetting like a river of flame through a cold blue sky.

She hurtled around the planet at a reckless speed, flashing overseas and islands and ice and vast green and brown plains.

She roared from high noon into midnight and out once more into the golden sparkle of a morning sun.

The drive suddenly broke off into a staccato series of blasts.

The ship began to vibrate and swing sickeningly from side to side.

"No more time left," yelled the navigator. "Everyone strap in and hang on to something that won't move, we're going down."

With a thunder that made the very mountains tremble, the ship that had come so far, turned its tail down, and rushed toward the ground in a geyser of flame toward her last and final landing place.

It went down toward a green world, third from its sun.

It went down toward Earth.

***

The ship came down, shattering the silence. Below her a marshy rolling plain of tough grass and wiry shrubs and amazingly vivid wild flowers disappeared in a scorching cloud of smoke and steam.

The ship was coming fast, too fast.

The braking jets were firing furiously but not very accurately.

The tongue of searing flame below the ship grew shorter and shorter, like a telescope slipping into itself.

The noise was incredible, a blast of overpowering, crashing sound that rushed out and smacked into the plains like a granite fist.

For just a moment the ship hung there poised, a scant few feet above the ground.

Then she dropped with a sudden jerk, slammed tail first into soft earth with a wet, shuddering concussion.

The ship seemed to fight for balance for a second or two, and then she buckled and collapsed on her side.

There were a few soft and muffled explosions, a flicker of intense white flames surrounding the spilled fuel around the crash site and then nothing.

The fires hissed themselves out almost immediately.

The ship quietly settled down as a broken, twisted thing, dying far from the stars she had known.

***

Silence came back to the flat plains area where the ship had settled, and the warm yellow sunlight flowed down from a blue morning sky.

The sunlight touched the reds and blues and golds of the flowers scattered through the clumps of tall grass.

A shocked peace returned to the land, a hush unbroken by the song of a bird or the snort of an animal.

Inside the downed ship, the emergency lights began to turn up and light up the interior areas. What they shined down upon was a complete disaster.

Almost everything that was not secured and tightened down had flown across the various rooms and smashed against the walls. The interior of the ship is one great big mess right now.

There was glass and broken items everywhere but no one took a direct hit from flying objects.

The Navigator who was looking at everyone on the internal computer screens, said to the Captain, with great relief in his voice, "Thanks to the Gods who are looking down on us, Captain."

The Crew Chief says everyone seems to be all right. There are some bumps and bruises but everyone seems to be pretty much OK, and I can see on my computer, some images showing that everyone is up and about and that verifies the Chiefs report.

The Chief said that they are all making their way out the side emergency exit that landed in a perfect position for easy in and out access.

I told the Chief to have everyone leave the ship together and keep them in a tight group. No one is to be allowed to wander away.

And Captain, the computer also tells me that the emergency engine had also shut itself down and that means that we seem to be in no danger from explosions or fire.

And now Captain, before we join the crew outside, shouldn't we pull up the final mapping charts and see what the computer is telling us about the land that is surrounding us.

We should determine where we are, and where it is that we want to be on this planet."

CHAPTER SEVEN

They sat in a circle on the sunward side of the ship, out of the cold wind that was blowing.

Even seated on the ground, the Captain dominated the small group.

He was by no means a big man, but he was the man you watched if only because of his tightly controlled energy.

He was a coiled spring, ready to go at the slightest touch.

He was their leader in fact as well as in theory, and he led because he was hard and tough.

The Captain had asked Wyat the Navigator to do the talking at this first and most important meeting. He realized that his first officer was closer to the rest of the party than he was, and that he could explain things to them in a much softer and easier to digest manner than he could.

After a brief nod from the captain, Wyat began to speak:
"The captain has asked me to explain our situation to everyone, and I'll try to make it as clear as I possibly can.

"In his wisdom, the captain ordered us to make a final sweep of the planet so that we could get a first-hand look at what this planet has to offer us.

"The first question that we asked the ship's computer before it shut down, was if there was anywhere on this world that we could get help so that we could put together another ship to take us home.

"The computer said 'absolutely not.'"

"The computer said that there was no advanced technology anywhere on the planet. It was very clear and precise in making this statement.

"The computer said that there are humans here on the planet but they are not too numerous as of yet. It is still fairly early in their development.

"And this is basically our main problem. We are many generations early in man's history on this planet. They have not even developed agriculture yet.

"In other words, we have landed in the middle of a 'stone age' world."

"The people are mostly scattered in small groups, living by hunting wild animals and gathering wild plant food like roots and berries and things like that.

"If we want to find out how to fix a broken spear point or something, we've come to the right place.

"But, if we want to know how to repair a spaceship, we'll have to wait about twenty thousand years or so, and then ask somebody.

"Except that, that somebody will probably be blowing himself up by then."

There was a long silence as the crew members merely sat quietly and looked at each other. There was little if any expression on their faces.

It was the crew chief who spoke up. "Wyat, what you and the captain are saying is that we are definitely stuck here on this back-water planet in the middle of nowhere. Is this correct?"

"I wouldn't quite put it that way chief, but you have it pretty much the way it is. We do have several options open and available to us."

"These options are just exactly what? What has the computer said about what is ahead of us," asked Alexa.

"Great question, Alexa.

"The computer told me that the long-range radio frequency was still operational, and I ordered it to send out our coordinates along with an emergency call for immediate assistance.

"The computer advised me that it had completed the task and that the message was on its way.

"It calculated that at the speed of light, which is186,000 miles per second, it would take several lifetimes for the message to arrive at our home planet since it will not be going through the distortion field like we normally do.

"Of course, that means that we are shipwrecked here for better or worse.

"It won't be until many, many years when we can expect any one to receive the message as well as respond to it. And who knows what will be happening on our home planet at that time?

"This means that we have to look after our own survival, and not expect any help from anywhere.

"I personally asked the computer how our entire company, which includes the captain and myself, compares in intelligence with the stone age humanoids who are roaming around the planet.

"The comparison came back stating that based upon what the computer understood about humans at this stage of development, that all of us are head and shoulders above them.

"To them, we are the equivalent of gods.

"Now being thought of as gods, is not really a bad thing. If we think this through, we could find ourselves much better off than we are at this exact moment in time.

"The good thing here, is that we can out think the locals, and our technology would easily give us the god-like appearances that would set us apart, and put us on top of the local food chain, as that old saying goes.

"The worst part of all of this is that none of us will live to see if this world survives.

"It will have to be our children and their children, etc., etc., who will finally see if this world survives atomics or blows itself up like everyone else.

"Even though we will have god and goddess status, we will still have to live, eat, fight and make love with the general population. It is only in the long run that our advanced gene pool will upgrade mankind.

"In order to keep who and what we are separate from the general population out there, we will have to mate a great deal among ourselves, and that will put a great deal of terrible pressure upon our nineteen-year-old, and very valuable female, Alexa.

"If we do this right, we all can have a decent life here among the primitives.

"Our children, and our children's children, and so on, should be able to rule this world as kings and queens.

"Our decedents could be the absolute rulers of this entire world, and if we play this out the right way, we can make this planet into a paradise, according to our own views of what paradise should be like.

"We will probably have to form some sort of a secret society that we all must conform to, so that when we finally go our separate ways in a few years, we will all know where it is that we are heading. None of us will ever be alone.

"The computer also tells us that we will have full use of all the tools, weapons, food, and anything else that we will need in the immediate future to insure our survival.

"And now, I am suggesting that we all find someplace within the ship to sleep tonight.

"We don't want to find out what is out there surrounding us this very moment. The best thing we can do is lock ourselves up tightly within the ship and get a good night sleep.

"Unless there are questions that cannot wait until tomorrow, the captain and I bid you all a good night, and make your last thought before you drift off to sleep, the pleasant thought that the future, if we all stick together, will be a good place for all of us."

CHAPTER EIGHT

Morning arrived and after everyone had eaten a basic breakfast aboard the ship, they all had assembled on a nearby grassy area within easy walking distance.

The weather *was* extremely pleasant with a reported temperature of seventy-eight degrees, and with a touch of a cooling breeze.

The group *was* sitting quietly as they waited for the Captain or Wyat to pick up the conversation from where they had left off yesterday.

Everyone, including Alexia, *was* wearing standard issue working clothes and comfortable shoes.

No one knew what their leaders had in mind to tell them, and they were suitably dressed for whatever they might have to do following the meeting.

It was the Captain who was standing next to several large printed, mounted maps.

Each of the mounted maps had the huge computer symbol imprinted at the top of each display board.

The Captain took a moment and gave each of them a smile, and once he saw that they had all settled down and that he had their full attention, he began to speak in his usual soft voice:

"The computer tells us that the humanoids walking around on this planet today, are to be called man the wise.

"I do not know if the computer which definitely has a limited sense of humor, is joking with me.

"It said 'man the wise' translates into a class of humanoids called 'Homo sapiens.'"

"Hereafter we shall call the stone age humans by that name. To us they will be Homo sapiens or human beings if you prefer.

"The reason for this name, at this time, is that there was another kind of humanoid walking around called Homo neanderthal, and the computer wants to separate the two Humanoid species.

"The Neanderthal is no longer present on this world and the computer image of what it believes he looked like is very interesting.

"The computer believes that the Neanderthal who preceded the Homo sapiens human, spent thousands of years sharing the world with the new comer, and then very suddenly disappeared.

"Evidence tell us that these humans that we will be seeing around us shortly, mated with Neanderthals many thousands of generations ago.

"Important swaths or characteristics of the bigger, stronger and older Neanderthals were given to Homo sapiens, when female humans mated with male Neanderthals.

"It is not clear if the mating was mutually agreed upon or not, but the computer suggested that when fighting occurred between humans and Neanderthals, female humans were taken captive by the Neanderthal where they acted as slaves.

"Of course, the females were raped and whenever a child was born of that union, some Neanderthal differences were transferred to the new breed of child.

"Neanderthal DNA that remain in today's humans include genes that altered hair and pigment of the skin, as well as others that strengthened the immune system.

"The computer offers these intriguing hints about how Neanderthal genes may have helped these Homo sapiens adapt as they spread around the world.

"An estimated 1% to 3% of the human make-up comes from the ancient Neanderthals, suggesting that members of the two related species mated perhaps for three hundred generations beginning about 50,000 years ago.

"The computer says that there is no way to tell if those encounters all happened about the same time or were actually spread out over the many generations that led up to today's humanoids.

"It is assumed that the crossbred children of human female and male Neanderthal would have been taller and stronger than the original humans who rarely grew to five and a half feet in height.

"This interbreeding probably gave female offspring, the ability to have permanently larger breasts than their contemporary human females.

"It is a known and well established fact, that early human females were depicted as having been very flat chested.

"It must be remembered that early man was basically no different from the Homo sapiens running around out there today, or even from us, the survivors of our ship wreck.

"Girls with bigger breasts get more attention, and probably got pregnant more often than the smaller chested female.

"Larger breasted women have always been more attractive to the male of the species, and therefore in prehistoric days such as we find ourselves today, will probably be the first choice for mating.

"The computer made one final theory before it lost all power and became useless.

"The computers second and last theory, held that "man the wise" or today's human beings, were much more aggressive than the bigger and slower Neanderthals.

"It is believed that these aggressive humans, hunted down and with the advanced invention of the human bow and arrow, the entire line of Neanderthals was wiped off the face of the planet.

"The following picture was computer generated to show us what the combination of Neanderthal and the human male should look like when we encounter them.

"The male looks formidable and quite dangerous, so caution is the wise way to approach them."

CHAPTER NINE

A much calmer and softer seeming Captain, paused in his speech to allow the rest of the crew to digest the important things he had just told them.

He was trying to come to terms with the calmness that had come upon him since he had safely crash landed the space craft that had taken all of them to this far away and pleasant seeming world.

He no longer would be responsible for the moment to moment happening to everyone in the crew. He would finish up his reports this morning and then step away from giving orders.

He felt almost happy with just knowing that he would shortly be just one more member of the shipwrecked crew who would have to scratch and fight their way into a new way of life.

He felt a tremendous relief for not being responsible for everyone and everything that went on.

His ship soon would exist no more in all of their lives, and he would be absolutely free of all responsibility. His only responsibility would be to himself and the survival of the people who would now become friends instead of crew members.

His spirits soared with the thoughts of the future that were flying through his mind as he cleared his throat to regain the attention of everyone who were now engaged in individual conversations.

"Hello, hello again everyone. I have a few more things to go over with you before I give up my position as captain, so please listen up.

"It is my thought that since Wyat and I are to step away from our command positions, since there no longer will be a ship to command, we all shall be equals after I finish up in a few minutes.

"I know that I speak for Wyat and myself, when I say that being one of you, my fellow shipwrecked friends, will be the adventure of a life time for all of us.

"Before I go into the maps and suggestions given to us by the computer before it went silent, I wish to call upon our beautiful reporter Alexa who has asked if she could share a few thoughts with us all.

"And before I forget, after this meeting is over, I would appreciate all of you calling me by my first name. I do have one, you know.

"If you want to call me captain, that will be fine since you are used to calling me that, but my preference would be to use my name which is Adam.

"And now gentlemen, I give you the most beautiful and charming of all of us, I give you Alexa."

The smiling and graceful former reporter, stood still for a moment as she slowly looked around at the friends she had shared so many friendly, funfilled, and sometime intimate moments with.

She was also feeling a sense of freedom just as she knew everyone else on the crew, including Navigator Wyat and the Captain (she knew she would have trouble thinking of the Captain as Adam) was feeling.

She had played reporter as she was getting acquainted with the crew during the beginning months of their now ill-fated explorations.

Except for the Captain who she never really talked to on a personal level, she found that each and every one of them, herself included, wanted to get away from the everyday boredom of life back home.

They were all seeking something new and exciting out of the voyage they had signed up for.

And now suddenly, here they were with something that was new and exciting and even scary, A SHIPWRECK.

From what Navigator Wyat and the Captain were telling them, this new world could be a rough and ready paradise for all of them if they stayed together and made things happen.

"Thank you captain.

"I know that I'm going to have a problem calling you Adam, because to me and to probably everyone else, you will always be our captain.

"But we will all try to honor your request and so Adam it will be.

"I like your thought of doing something new to start off our lives on this world that we seem to have inherited.

"I am also going to change my home world name of Alexa. I would like to use my middle name for who I shall become in my new life on this planet.

"I would like to also leave my old name of Alexa behind with the spaceship that we shall soon abandon.

"Kindly try to forget my first name of Alexa, and just use my middle name.

"I will always answer to Alexa of course, but I have always loved my middle name.

"So please call me "Eve.""

CHAPTER TEN

Alexa, or as she now became to be known as Eve, continued.

"I put together this morning, page one of the daily journal that I plan to keep for all of us.

"I have entered a few thoughts that have come to me here upon this lovely new world of ours.

"Please give me a few moments to share my words with you all.

"Nearly a hundred thousand million stars are turning in the circle of our vast milky way galaxy.

"Long ago, other races on other worlds of other suns must have achieved and passed the heights that we recently reached on our home planet Enaid.

"Think of such civilizations, far back in time against the fading afterglow of creation.

"They were masters of a universe so young, that life had come only to a handful of worlds.

"The people of those civilizations would have loneliness that we can't imagine.

"It would have been like the loneliness of gods and goddess's looking out across infinity and finding none to share their thoughts.

"They must have searched the star clusters as we have, and found planets like we did.

"They would have found them empty or peopled with crawling mindless things.

"And now here we are, searchers and wanderers, who look on this planet which navigator Wyat called "Earth," as a haven for us and our children to follow.

"We look upon this planet "Earth" which is circling safely in the narrow zone between solar fire and deep space ice, and guess that this will be the planet that will someday join our ancestral home in a union that will transform the entire universe.

"This is a world where everything is hauntingly familiar, but never quite the same.

"This is a world that we hope will join our home world, and provide a future for all of mankind, no matter where their lives began.

"We hope and pray that this planet earth, will fulfill all of our hopes and dreams for the future of the human race, no matter where they may be.

"Thank you all for listening."

CHAPTER ELEVEN

The Captain picked up the conversation.

"Our ship crash-landed here on this detailed map that I am now holding up before you.

"This is an area that will someday be called Asia.

"The computer said that we should not stay here and we would be right in asking ourselves why not?

"We are already here, and everything in this neighborhood seems to be working in our favor.

"The climate seems right, the plant and animals that we need for our food supply seem ample, so why not stay here?

"The reason why not to stay is rather simple. This "Asian" area is out of the edge of where the planet will begin to develop its civilizations.

"The most intensive and positive development of advanced culture on this planet earth, seems to be here."

His finger touched a part of what in time would be called Paris.

"Let me step away from this Paris area for the moment and talk about other possible sites for us to settle.

"There is a lot of small tribal activity scattered all through this region and down south of it into a large land mass called a continent."

He indicated Africa, "When agriculture develops, it should come first, somewhere between these two major areas."

He drew an imaginary line between Africa and Europe of which France was in the very center.

"Perhaps somewhat closer to that huge body of water would be a little more accurate."

He drew his imaginary line, and ended up at the Mediterranean Sea.

Navigator Wyat interjected, "Was the computer suggesting that we should try to get ourselves over to that seaside area?"

"You are close," Wyat, "but the computer is more devious than that.

"The Mediterranean area is where human growth populations will be concentrated over a long time.

"If we are going to build ourselves as a separate and much more advanced civilization over the centuries, then we need to find an area that will blossom suddenly when new ideas hit."

Wyat asked again, "Is there such an area where we can either wait for our rescue, and live out our lives at the same time in luxury and comfort?"

"The computer does not tell us for sure, but it has eliminated few places that we should not go, and that makes things a bit easier.

"For example, this huge island here, would not be a good place. It seems to be mostly desert." His fingers touched the island men would one day call Australia.

His hand then swept over a number of the pacific islands, "These are too small and impossible for us to get to unless we wanted to risk it in a boat of some sort, so we can rule these out. But I want you to look at this area that the computer printed out as bright green."

The captain's finger traced the outline of the continental mass that would thousands of years later challenge the imagination of men as they referred to it as the new world or America.

"Is it inhabited now?"

"I don't know, it seems that man did not evolve there on this planet and there certainly is not a great population there at this time.

"I don't see hardly any image of man on the readout but we can be sure that a few have arrived. But let me call your attention to what the computer said will be happening there."

Everyone walked over and looked at the displayed paperwork that was in front of the captain, but it seemed to give them no information.

It appeared to them to be just a lot of dots, lines and swirls.

The captain saw their puzzled look.

"OK," he said. "let me explain what you are looking at in more detail.

"There will be small groups of humans that will get into this huge area from different directions.

"This location called America, will be found to be rich in land, well-watered and as an enormously untouched continent.

"These early men will come to America from Europe across an area of land that will appear out of the usual water that covers it over.

"The present ice age that the planet is now going through, will cause water to fall back as it is absorbed in large masses of ice that will be forming all around it.

"This land will stay dry for a few hundred years which will be long enough for the humans to use it as a connecting path from Europe to America.

"The Bering strait will again disappear under water in later years when the ice begins to melt again, but by then there will be enough population for us to do what we will be doing.

"This will be both good and bad for our needs.

"This means that there will be a limited but fairly good sized amount of people for us to work with.

"When the area finally is cut off again by the melting ice, we will be able to produce an advanced civilization that will be cut off from the rest of the world.

"It is important that we allow the rest of the world to develop at their own pace and be completely free from any interference from us.

"Our immediate problem that we now face is getting ourselves over to the America continent from where we are here in central Asia. It is a walking distance of several thousand miles and will take years to get there even with the help of locals.

"Some of the equipment we will want to take with us will have to be broken up into parts that we can reassemble when we arrive at our final destination.

"Once we get to America we can pretty much set up our systems and disappear underground just the way we want to.

"We will have to be good at hiding ourselves away from the rest of the world, but we have generations of time to make our disappearance.

"We can easily make our new homes prosper as we wait for the Europeans to cross the ocean and blunder into America on their own.

"These Europeans will find a virtually untouched paradise, and they will, of course, take it away from the original settlers who we will call Indians.

"Once this new land of America is settled by the Europeans, they should begin to make rapid advancement in the sciences.

"If this holds true, we will then be able to make ourselves known to them and hopefully we can stop them from blowing themselves up.

"We have to be very careful to instill in our special line of decedents, a desire to lead our adopted world, which we will call planet Earth. Hopefully they will become the leaders of this planet.

"And finally, maybe, just maybe, by the time all of these things begin to happen, our cousins from our old planet, will come here to visit us in order to see what happened to their old universal explorers.

"When they come, and I truly believe that they will come, they probably will not make themselves known right away.

"They will probably put themselves in the depths of the ocean or on the side of the moon whose side never turns toward the earth, and build their first bases there.

"I am assuming they will stay around for a long time to see if we can avoid blowing up our world, and if they like what they see, they will no longer stay hidden.

"They no longer will be aliens to our world. They will make themselves welcomed as our sister planet representatives, then, the two worlds, working together will be able to achieve everything that possible."

CHAPTER TWELVE

One of the crew members who had been silent through all the time that the Captain was speaking, got slowly to his feet and shielded his eyes from the sun.

"Captain, Sir. Before we make too many plans about living with the natives, perhaps we'd better ask them directly, because a few of them are headed our way."

The others all came to their feet and looked outward in the direction that the crew member was pointing.

There, coming across the plains from the south, were dark figures. They were silent, but moving rapidly toward them.

Everyone was aware of the facts that whatever else could be said about "man", one very basic thing to remember, was that "man" was always dangerous.

Man, was the supreme killer animal, and even man's own kind faced other men at their own peril.

"Calm down," the Captain said. "Wyat, he whispered. Please go inside and get out small stun guns. The rest of you stand perfectly still and wait for Wyat to come back and arm all of us. Do not make any sudden moves.

"Are stone age men cannibals?" whispered Alexa to one of the others.

"Listen up," said the Captain. We don't know anything about

them up close and personal as we will be in another few minutes."

"We've got to find out if we can get along with them. I don't see any great danger from those four men and a dog approaching us. Our guns will be far better by far than anything they've got with them."

As Wyat passed out the guns to everyone, the Captain said in a firm voice, "No one will fire unless we are attacked and only upon my order. Everyone please stand down.

The four men who were walking across the plains toward them, were as silent as the wind.

They had a shaggy wolf/dog with them, and the dog began barking at them as they drew nearer.

They all watched the natives approaching with a sense of awe and wonder. This would be their first encounter with off-world people since they had left their home planet a long time ago.

The figures moved closer, walking steadily and with no effort at concealment.

They could almost make out the details of the men that they were looking at, but not quite yet.

For the Captain and the crew, it was like looking into the past, staring into that vast and shadowed fog that was the cradle of man on many worlds.

Approaching them now, were men who had never known cities, or agriculture or writing or any other civilized thing.

The contrast between their experiences and the crews, gave to the natives a kind of innocence.

As their lives progressed, they would know fear, selfishness and perhaps even horror. But they had yet to discover the evil that was within themselves.

They continued walking toward them, walking out of youth, and out of time itself. They stopped some thirty yards away the shipwrecked crew could see them clearly now.

They stood quietly in a line, silent and unafraid.

The dog that seemed to be mostly wolf, put his belly to the ground and whined, his pink tongue just dripping with saliva.

The reality of a meeting like this, as usual, was something of an anticlimax when seen up close.

And yet it had its own drama about it, the drama of sweat and hopes and smells.

The natives were not very tall. There was not a man among them that stood above five feet. Their hair which was dirty looking, was long, straight and black.

Their eyes were narrow and dark. Their skin was a yellowish bronze in color, and they were dressed in crudely sewn hides.

These men were proud men. They stood quite still and did not fidget at all.

They eyed the strangers with a frank curiosity, but with an assumed superiority that waited for them, the people from the strange vehicle, to make the first move.

They were armed. Two of them carried stone-tipped spears, and the two others carried a kind of throwing stick armed with a wicked looking tip.

The wind shifted and the crew caught a whiff of them, and wished they hadn't.

Washing was not yet one of their best habits.

CHAPTER THIRTEEN

The Captain whispered to Wyat, "Go into the ship and get four sharp knives from the lunch area. When you get back, you and I will go out there and see if we can make some friends."

Wyat ducked into the ship as the natives watched silently. What did they make of the ship? How could they explain it to each other?

The Captain tried to follow the thought process that the natives would be going through. They were intelligent enough, of course, to know the ship was not a natural object from their world.

Would they be able to connect the ship with the loud thunder that must have shattered their world a few days back?

Wyat came back with the knives.

The two officers walked slowly toward the natives and watched the dog leap to its feet and bristle at their approach.

The four natives lifted up their weapons in a very threatening manner.

The Captain held a sharp kitchen knife in each hand, griping them carefully by their points so that the handles were pointing toward the natives. Wyat did the same with the other two knives.

To the natives who were watching them very carefully, their intent must have been obvious because they immediately lowered their weapons.

The dog was still growling deep within its throat as Wyat and the Captain put the knives down on the grass and took several steps back.

Each officer was careful to keep a smile on his face, while they pointed to the natives and then to the gifts that they were giving to them.

The dark-eyed men seemed to be rather intelligent as one of the men, probably the leader, stepped forward and scooped up the knives with two hands.

He stared at them as he turned them over and over in his hands.

He decided to test the sharpness of the blade against the skin of his own arm and seemed quite startled when it drew blood.

The leader then held the knives up to the sunlight and watched it gleam as it caught the light.

He pointed at the two officers as if he was saying thank you. There was a big smile on his ugly face as he turned to the others in his party.

The other three natives moved up to the leader, looking chattering away in a language that was not understandable to the men from the stars.

The four of them were chattering away with much excitement in their voices as the leader suddenly stepped back and away from the other three.

The other three without the gifts, followed after him and were talking rapidly to him.

Obviously, the leader wanted to keep all the knives for himself, and equally obvious was the fact that the others were not too happy with that idea.

A first-rate argument promptly developed, and stopped only when the leader with the knives, after trying in vain to decide which one to keep for himself, divided up the other knives, giving one to each of the others.

Then they all got to laughing and reflecting the sunlight into each other's eyes with the shining metal blades.

They were good fun to watch and Wyat and the Captain found themselves laughing and enjoying the performance from where they were standing.

And then, incredibly, the four natives simply turned their backs on the ship and walked away with the dog bounding ahead of them.

They didn't look back at all and appeared to be utterly unconcerned.

Soon they were only shadows again, and then they were completely lost from view.

"Well, that was very interesting, wasn't it Captain.?"

"I guess we are not as important as we thought we were. We have just had a lesson in ego deflation."

The Captain shook his head at the Navigator. "They'll be back, Wyat. They will be back."

"How do you know that, Sir?"

The Captain suddenly looked older, as though a fraction of his tremendous energy had momentarily deserted him.

"They always come back, Wyat. They always come back one way or another."

CHAPTER FOURTEEN

The sun was high overhead and it was a beautiful day as the Captain sat on a flat raised rock, his small body comfortably slouched, his chin resting in his cupped hand.

The slight breeze that rustled through the grasses had a keen smell to it, but the sunlight was warm on his back.

There were patches of white clouds in the sky, and whenever one of them drifted across the face of the sun, it grew decidedly chilly.

He looked around and discovered somewhat to his own amazement, that he felt better than he had in many years.

The ship which was a hundred yards away in the middle of a circle of scarred vegetation and scorched earth, was crumpled but harmless.

In a few years, he knew that it would only be a shell, and within a century it would not exist anymore.

There would only be the plains, the gleaming-tipped mountains, and the winds that blew everywhere.

He felt a curious joy just in being outside, where he could breathe clean air and hear the long, living silences that washed in from far away.

He rejoiced in even the bugs that plodded dutifully through the grass, bound on pressing bug business.

He was more than ready for whatever might come at them. He was actually eager for it, even impatient for it, whatever "it" was.

He was thinking that a man was not born to live in a tube of steel.

A man was a part of the land and the sky.

His body had known that even when his mind reached out across the light years, into star fields and challenges and desolation.

He was lonely for his home world of Enaid, and the loneliness was accentuated by the fact that this planet was so much like it in many ways, even though they were separated from each other by a gulf of years as well as miles.

But he was not desperately lonely. He had friends and companions from home that helped ease the pain for him.

He was not proud of the life he had left behind him on Enaid. It had been too easy for him, and it had come too fast.

Too many pleasures, too many woman, too many nights that were so similar he could never tell them apart.

Even high living can get monotonous.

***

Another evening had passed and things were quiet during the night, and that made for a rested group of people who were once again assembled around the Captain.

They were here to decide upon the actions that they should be taking that would be responsible for the rest of their lives on the planet Earth.

It was Navigator Wyat who stood up in front of the group and started to speak for all of them.

"Captain, I took the time to meet with each and every member or our crew and we all agreed that we would be honored if you would continue to guide us as our elected leader for whatever lies ahead of us.

"There is no one among us who has any thoughts to do anything or go anywhere other than within the plan that you had previously suggested.

"In other words, Captain we would appreciate your staying on as our leader and planner. We would not know what to do if you weren't there to guide us.

"We would all feel better if you formally agreed to continue doing for us all, as you have been doing these many years that we have all been together.

"Can we hear an affirmative answer from you now, Sir?"

"All right, Wyat and the rest of you." the Captain said, "I accept your kind offer and I have to admit that I am humbled by your confidence in me.

"I think it is important now for us to get down to the business at hand. We spoke about where we should be going and how we would end up being thousands of miles away in that place that will be called America.

"And you are all correct about that being a walk way past a thousand miles of unknown dangers and pitfalls.

"We don't know what exactly lies ahead of us, but if we stick to our plan we know that the ultimate reward for all of us and for all of our children and grandchildren and so on, will be something wonderful.

"We all know the odds are overwhelmingly against this world ever attaining space travel, even in its most rudimentary form.

"The civilization here must be built by local men and women, and we have all seen, on world after world, that man characteristically destroys himself when he has the power to do so.

"If we do make it to this other part of the world, there is still a good chance that this planet is the planet that we have been looking for all these years.

"And even knowing that, it is a slim chance that this is the one, I still think that it is worth the effort after all, what else is there to do with our lives if we just take the easy way out and stay here?"

***

They slept inside the ship that night, and it was like sleeping in a tomb.

They posted no guard since once the air lock was shut, nothing could get at them.

But the ship itself had changed, at least in their minds. In only a few days, it had grown old, and it seemed to belong to the past.

There was not a man or woman in the ship that night, who did not think of that closed airlock door as something that was sealing them off forever from the sun and the freedom of the outdoors. It was amazing to them all, how quickly they had changed.

In the middle of the night, the Captain and Wyat the navigator worked out a plan for the best use of the small three-person scouting helicopter.

They would all take turns flying the helicopter which meant that once every ninth day each of them would be off their feet and resting in the pilot's seat and not having to walk with the rest of them. They would draw numbers to see the piloting schedule.

They would remove the extra two passenger seats from the helicopter and load that space up with the equipment from the ship that they would be taking with them.

The advanced equipment would consist of a ship board compass and computer to keep them on course, a mapping system to guide them with the shortest and easiest route to America, and all the rest of the weapons and advanced items that would insure their dominance over any humanoids they encountered.

They would also include several atomic digging devices for digging out their underground homes when they finally arrived at their destination.

And the most wonderful thing of all, was that the helicopter worked off of solar power and would never stop running. They would also pack repair parts for the motor and other moving parts to keep it running properly.

It was the helicopter that would make the journey possible and they realized how fortunate they were that it was not damaged during the crash landing.

CHAPTER FIFTEEN

The natives came with the rising sun.

There was something almost supernatural about their appearance. One minute the plains were empty of human life, and the next minute men were there, as though they had simply materialized out of the grass and rocks and morning wetness.

The natives brought meat with them, and there was nothing supernatural about that. They built a fire on the sheltered side of the ship, using what looked like dried dung chips for fuel, and roasted great chunks of red meat in the flames.

The meat sizzled and dripped, and it was simply wonderful eating it after long years of eating synthetic food stores.

"A trifle raw," one of the crew members commented, "but what's a little blood between friends?"

They threw a piece to the dog, who wolfed it down gratefully, belched, and settled down to a sensible nap in the sunlight.

The natives did not seem concerned by the fact that they could not understand the language of the men who lived in the strange tower.

Evidently, they had come across groups of men before who spoke tongues different from their own, and it was surprising how they could make themselves understood just by smiles and gestures.

They certainly seemed friendly enough, although it was always possible that they were just impressed by the knives and wanted more of them.

Looking at the rippling muscles in their arms and legs, and the jagged points on their spears, the entire crew was hoping that they would stay as friendly as they now were.

When breakfast was over, the leader stood up, stretched and pointed in a southern direction.

There, across the plains, the land grew more rolling and a low chain of hills were visible as they rose out of a purple tinged haze.

He pointed again to the hills, then to the crew and then back to the hills.

"He obviously wants us to go with him," Wyat said.

It was the only female member of the crew who laughingly commented "they've probably got the old stewpot bubbling and waiting for us."

This drew a subdued laugh from everyone and the natives smiled when the crew members smiled.

The Captain commented that he didn't think that it would be smart to refuse their hospitality after all they seemed to mean no harm.

Wyat and all the others nodded in agreement.

"All right, then it's settled. We'll take the walk with them, and then come back and see about getting ready to go to America."

"This side trip will be a good way for us to see firsthand what the living conditions are, and how advanced the natives are on the social scale."

"Everyone get armed with side arms and some extra ammunition in case we have to fight our way back. Bring a few more gifts from each of us. No more knives. Bring a flashlight, some trinkets and maybe some extra clothes. All right let's get started."

They got ready clambering through the ship with an *odd* sense of sadness.

Of course, they would be back, and the ship was a complete

ruin. Still it gave them all a funny feeling to leave their last real tie with home.

The natives watched with expressionless dark eyes. They saw the crew members climb in and out of the black tunnel in the shiny outside wall, but they made no attempt to follow them inside.

When they had loaded themselves up and put on warm clothes against the chill in the air, the Captain nodded and pointed toward the hills.

The natives grinned, as though pleased, and set off across the plains.

The dog was up in an instant and led the way. He didn't bark now, and kept his black muzzle to the ground.

The land was not as level as it looked. The grass which appeared to be very smooth from a distance was growing in bothersome clumps and the black soil was rocky and hard to walk on.

There were hidden depressions that caught at their ankles and thorny bushes that scraped at them as they walked by.

The natives seemed unconcerned about all these things, and they kept up a lively chatter among themselves as they set a brisk pace for the group.

Once they glimpsed a herd of animals ahead of them. They were beauties, large and delicately poised, with lovely brown coloring and tossing antlers.

But they were downwind from the men, and caught their scent long before they were in range of the dart throwers of the natives.

The animals milled around a bit, then a huge stag decisively snorted, and set out at a slow trot away from the humans' who were passing them by.

The entire herd followed him, not really running, but moving right along away from the walkers.

The leader of the natives pointed at the moving animals, said a word or two that the space travelers could not understand, and then called back the dog that had started out in eager pursuit.

They walked for hours, and the crew from the ship were tiring out rapidly.

Soon it would no longer be an exciting adventure. Soon they would have to stop and rest.

The land began to rise and they were suddenly on a definite path that wound into the nearby hills.

The hills were close up now and seemed fairly formidable.

They kept on walking.

Behind them and to the west, black clouds began to pile up in the sky, and the wind moaned down across the plains.

The grasses were moving in the wind like waves, and far off in the distance there was the rumble of thunder.

The natives kept chattering happily.

The crew from space stuck their heads down and kept on with it.

Within an hour, it was raining hard.

CHAPTER SIXTEEN

You don't notice scenery in the rain.

The water whirs and drums all around you, splashing on the rocks and digging tiny holes in the wet black earth.

Your hair is plastered down on your forehead, and water drips in your eyes, and you blink, and they get red and stingy.

Your clothes hang on your body like heavy felt sacks, and your own sweat makes you clammy and hot.

There is water in your shoes, gallons of it, and every time you take a step you feel your toes squishing, and occasionally you fall down.

You grab out for a tree but there are no trees.

Soon your face is cut a little, and it stings where the rain hits against it.

Then, incredibly, it is over.

***

One of the natives ahead of them cried out, and a woman's voice hollered something in return.

Their eyes brought everything back into focus again, and picked out a blur of warm yellow light in the gray haze.

They squinted and saw some roundish humps rising up out of

some sheltered high ground at the head of a small valley.

The humps turned out to be grass-woven living houses.

They stumbled on, and someone caught their arms and steered them toward a light.

They were guided through an opening, and almost fell as their feet missed a short flight of dirt stairs inside.

Sunken living room they thought.

But it was light, and warm.

***

There was a fire blazing strongly in the huge gathering area where the entire crew was now standing in a circle around the blaze.

One of the younger boys from the natives was feeding wood slowly into the fire to keep it at a level.

The smoke went straight upward into an opening left at the very center of the ceiling and surprisingly it made for good ventilation. This was a good sign for civilization and the housing market.

The crew gathered around the fire were given woven mats to sit on and sheepskin towels to dry themselves and their clothing.

It wasn't long before each of them, feeling much warmer and more secure, were sleeping around the warming fire.

They figured that they had walked at least twenty miles from the ship to get here and their muscles were not used to the effort.

It was only the Captain who was not sleeping as he sat there quietly watching over his people as they all slept.

The night was beginning to fade into the sky, and with it the rainfall moved away as the leader of the walking group of natives, bounded into the room and went up to the Captain and the two of them with many gestures and pointing, came to an understanding.

Moments later, the native smiled at the Captain and left the tent where it was quiet as the Captain let the crew members get a few more hours of much needed sleep.

He also allowed himself the luxury of several catnaps before his watch alarm went off and woke everyone up in the room.

"Hello everyone. I hope you all had a nice nap. You have all been asleep about three hours, and it is time for us to tidy ourselves up and look our best because we have just been invited by the tribal chief to a party being given in our honor."

My watch which is set to shipboard time, tells me that it is almost four o'clock in the morning. Let's take an hour or so and then gather ourselves in the center of this little village which is the big hut that dominates the city square. You can't miss it."

With a big smile on his face, the Captain left them all to clean themselves up and went and sat at one of the nearby fires as he watched the night fall and the stars light up the sky.

He was trying to pick out some of the star constellations in the sky that he remembered from the star charts when he was pleasantly interrupted by the beautiful reporter who sat down quietly beside him.

They smiled at each other and just sat there enjoying the quiet of the moment and each other's company. It was most pleasant for the two of them who wished now to be known as Adam and Eve.

It was about an hour later when all nine crew members walked into the central tribal gathering hut and spread themselves around the room.

The Captain and Eve found themselves chatting with each other and watching the goings on around them.

It appeared that most of the natives that were present were female members of the tribe and not surprisingly the loin clothes and loose fitting tops left little if anything to the imagination.

At least two females were being attentive to each member of the crew and all seven of the men seemed to be having a wonderful time with the mostly naked girls.

Adam and Eve laughed as one by one, each crew member and the females with them, quietly left the party and headed for a smaller and more private hut where they could have their own private party.

It was Adam who remarked to a laughing Eve, that the tribe's gene pool would get some new donations to the mix tonight.

It was quiet in the big hut as the Captain and his new friend spent the hours away talking about home, friends and what the future might hold for them all. It was a most pleasant evening, and when they finally said good night to the Natives leader, they went back to the original hut where they had first warmed themselves by the fire after their long walk.

It was only at that moment that they both realized that they were completely alone with each other and no one else would be coming along for many hours.

CHAPTER SEVENTEEN

Eve smelled good to him.

It was a sweet exotic and tingling sensation of a smell that pleased Captain Adam very much.

She was like a very special flower that blooms in the sunshine and only opens to be seen and admired.

It was easy for Adam to put the crew, the new plans and the exciting days that lay before them away from his mind just then, as he was alone with her for the first time.

They had no eyes for the interior of the rough community hut, and they do not notice the dirty interior or the chill in the air as the warming fire of earlier that evening was almost completely out.

They are only aware of each other; and nothing else will detract them as each of them can hardly wait for the intimate moments that they both know are coming.

Slowly he slides his fingers under her beautiful chin, moving inch by inch toward her right ear. Adam is taking great personal pleasure in this first and most important intimate contact with her skin.

The very texture of her is as smooth and velvety as it has always looked to him, as he feels the fire and heat coming from her closely pressed body, and he senses, in a deep down and very primitive way, the simmering heat of her needs.

He touches her earring, which is a simple designed piece of jade, and then he caresses her lobe, tucking back her long dark hair.

Like a smoothly moving cat, she turns her cheek into his moving fingers.

Leaning down from the few inches that he has on her in height, he kisses her lightly with a mere brush of his lips upon hers.

He only wants the slightest taste of her in this brief exchange, and with this taste the lightest touching of their lips to heighten her desire. He knows he wants more, much more of this special female.

He presses his fingers to her full lips as he softly says, I'll try not to smear your lipstick too much. I'll be very careful."

A sly smile plays across her lips and, with a special twinkle in her eyes, she replies in the softest of voices, "my makeup artist, back on our Planet Enaid, promised me that when all the rest of me has turned to dust, the lipstick will be the only thing left of me. You see, I have had them permanently done."

Captain Adam gave her a big grin. In her own way, Eve was quite funny and very interesting.

She does not smile back at him. She is simply stating a fact. She presses her hand to his chest, a very firm touch filled with her determination.

"I would like a kiss," she says quietly. "A real kiss this time because I want to know if it will be as good as I think it will be."

A deliberate challenge, perhaps, Adam is thinking, or quite possibly, she is being sincere. Certainly, love has cheated her somehow in her past, and honestly, I am only one of eight choices of mates that she has to choose from among the crew.

He is still smiling as he leans towards her again, and gives her what she wants. Lips are parted and tongue meets tongue.

For the first time in many years, this first kiss completely shuts out the real world for them both.

Suddenly there are just the two of them as each one is excited by the touch of the others lips.

Adam realizes that there is something special going on here, and he wants to explore these sensations to the fullest.

She closes her eyes as he kisses her again so that she could better savor the taste of him. He tastes of strong male-ness and power and tenderness and the strength that she had always looked for in a male companion.

Adam closed his eyes as he kisses her again to better savor the taste of her.

She tastes somewhat of sweet brown sugar and it was a good taste.

To him she was simply wonderful, like a fluffy cream candy melting with obvious warm desires.

She also sent visions into his mind of a very fine wine, something very grand, expensive and very much worth each delicious taste.

He forgets about deliberation. He forgets about restraint. He pulls her closely against himself, crushing her to him.

His other hand slides beneath the nape of her neck to hold her in place. He bends her back a little bit, holding her weight against him as he experiences who she is through her mouth and through her soft and giving body that she presses tightly up against his, and through the special smell of her that seems to be inside his pounding head.

The age-old primitive man part of him fights for dominance.

The instinct that ancient man has passed down to modem man for generations beyond counting, tells him to rip her clothes off and take her right there and then.

A lifetime of civilized ways, quickly overrules the lust that is now thundering through his body.

Stepping back to allow some space between them, he quickly removes his shirt and puts his arms around her yielding waist once again.

She looks at him carefully, and takes his arms from where they were. "I want you Adam, and I want you now."

She kicks off her hiking boots and slowly and teasingly begins to remove her clothing.

First comes the black and white outer jacket that was standard issue for all crew members. Then she removes the long, black belt that is attached at her waist. She simply throws it away from her.

Next, she slowly and tantalizingly removes her black leather jeans and throws them on top of her shoes just a few feet away.

In a matter of seconds, the black turtle-necked long sleeved shirt becomes part of the rumpled mess that is growing on the floor all around them.

Adam stands there without realizing that a primitive growling is coming from his throat.

She is standing before him looking like, but much better than, the pictures of female models that he had kept in his private cabin all of these years.

Eve is now smiling a reserved Mona Lisa smile as she reaches behind her back and unhooks the bra that holds her magnificent breasts for him to see.

As the bra hits the floor, her hands drop to his belt which she quickly pulls out of their restraining loops and drops it to the floor.

With experienced hands, she unbuttons the buttons on his shirt and then unzips his pants, allowing them to fall into the pile of nearby clothing that is growing rapidly.

THE LADY IS ON FIRE.

Her hands drag across his erection and she feels its heat through the layer of cloth that is his undershorts.

Her heart is now pounding within her as she asks herself what it will be like to feel that heat deeply within her.

Her anticipation is so great that every inch of her being feels flushed beyond control.

Adam easily picks her up, carries her into the large sectioned-off bedroom and deposits her down on the native's version of a large bed.

His fingers skim up to the lacy elastic band of her sheer panties.

Within moments, the last of all their remaining clothing joins the growing pile of discarded items.

Within moments, Eve is beginning to shiver from the coldness of the air and the heat being generated by his hands as they roam freely over her body.

She is savoring the sheer ecstasy of his touch and in the heat of the moment, she spreads her legs and pulls him towards her.

He is so close that she can smell the passion that seems to be steaming off his skin.

This is acting like an aphrodisiac upon her and she arches up to him.

She gave herself up to the wild, mindboggling sensations that made her realize that she had come to life for the very first time.

She had been to bed with many other men because there was nothing shy about her. She wanted to experience what sex was all about and she had surely had her share of experiences.

But she was now astonished by the maelstrom of emotions that she had never experienced with any other man, and she found herself wanting more and more of her new lover.

She gasped like a schoolgirl who was experiencing love making for the first time. She had problems catching her breadth when his caresses became far more urgent and definitely more erotic as he spent a few moments playing with her breasts and forcefully sucking at her nipples which puckered out to meet his demanding mouth.

He guided her thighs apart with his knees, and bent to spread a row of heated kisses over her stomach and the curve of her hips.

When his hands glided lower, Eve completely forgot how to breathe or why she needed to. These never before sensations were her body responding to a master player of all her feminine parts.

Her body shuddered in uncontrollable spasms when his fingertips began to explore the very essence of her femininity.

He stroked her, aroused her, until she convulsed around him, lost in sweet torturous pleasure.

Suddenly his intimate caresses were not enough to satisfy the monstrous ache that was swallowing her alive.

Eve clutched at him, her nails digging into the very scars on his shoulders.

Adam had depleted every ounce of self-restraint that he possessed. He intentionally held back from entering her as long as he could. He knew that other men had been where he was now, but he wanted to do something different to her that would be remembered as special between them.

And so, he had held back from entry as long as he could. He had held back until he knew by the passion she was showing, that she was more than ready for him. He would torture her no more once he had made her desire him beyond all others with his extended love making, and now this was the moment.

As for Eve, who was in the heat of the moment as Adam thrust deeply into her tender flesh, the world began exploding into colors and sensations that she had never experienced before.

It was as if this was her first lover as the steady rocking motion began to penetrate her—deeper and deeper and she was loving it.

A hoarse cry tumbled from her lips but Adam smothered it with his possessive kiss, sharing his breadth when she could grasp none of her own.

And then, suddenly, an exquisite pleasure born of pain and pleasure flooded completely over her.

Eve could feel herself accepting his deep entry like a new blossom unfolding in the warmth of the morning sun.

She began to move in rhythm with him, meeting each hard-penetrating thrust of his with a rocking motion of her own.

She felt as if she was being consumed by a ball of fire that consumes all within its path, feeding on its own raging flames.

She lost every ounce of self-control that she had as a wild spasm raced through every nerve and muscle. She was clinging to Adam as if he were the only force in the swirling universe, and indeed, at that moment, to her he was.

She was living and dying in the same fantastic moment.

When his powerful body shuddered upon hers, another wave of sensations crested over her, stripping every last fragment of thought from her mind.

For what seemed like forever, Eve laid there, her body intimately joined with him as if she were a living and breathing part of this incredible man.

A lazy smile pursed her lips as her hand absently trailed across his hip to investigate the corded muscles of his back.

How very easy, she thought, to fall in love with a man such as this.

On those contented thoughts, Eve drifted off to sleep to relive in her dreams, the erotic events that she had just experienced.

She could vividly see those twinkling blue-gray eyes of his, just reaching out to her across a sea of delicious memories.

***

Several weeks had passed and no one brought up the subject of getting back to the ship and undertaking the trip across the continent to the promised land called America.

Every single one of the crew had found someone special to spend their days and nights with in the small native compound, but this small touch of Paradise was about to end.

It all happened one night after everyone had been gathered outside in the center open court area having their evening dinner.

The various couples were all wandering off when terror struck that quiet little area in the form of blood-curling screams that shattered the night.

Suddenly there were flames to be seen everywhere.

Everyone jumped every which way. A thrown spear thudded into the ground near the Captain's feet.

Screaming and yelling erupted everywhere as local men and women toppled with large spears driven through their bodies.

The bonfires hissed as blood spattered onto them.

The friendly natives ran for their huts, terrified but not the Captain and crew members who stood their ground waiting for orders.

"Get your guns," the Captain was shouting. "Get your weapons from your hut and return fire. Be sure not to hit our friends since they all look alike in the dark."

The Captain and Eve began running together toward their living area, and as they ran they could see by the firelight, the attacking almost completely naked humans who had their faces painted in hideous colors as they dashed into and out of the various huts.

Some of the attackers held torches and others held sharply pointed spears.

The firelight glinted off the enemy's bodies, and that added to the illusion and confusion of the moment.

All of this was happening in seconds as Adam rushed into the hut with Eve right behind him.

Adam knocked down an enemy warrior who was searching the inside of the hut and was able to twist his neck until he heard it snap.

Eve was able to find her gun and ammunition which she had left in a far comer of the hut, but Adam could not find his pistol and reloads where he had left them.

With no hesitation at all, he took the quiver full of arrows from off the body of the fallen warrior and took the bow that was lying next to his body.

He ordered Eve to take a position just inside the entrance to the hut and to fire at anyone she did not know who tried to enter. He ordered her not to leave the tent and her years of training kicked in and she followed his orders and took up her position at the inside of the entrance.

Knowing that Eve would be safe for the moment, Adam darted back into the night air outside of his hut, side-stepping to avoid an enemy warrior who sprang at him with a spear leveled at his chest.

Adam floored the warrior with a lethal punch to his neck.

He stepped over the floored warrior's body and stepped out into the flame-filled screaming furor of the battle, with every one of his senses alert and sharpened to its finest pitch.

Adam felt a wild exhilaration. The dullness that his life had become was now over for him, and the battle going on around him was ready for him to join.

His spirit soared with the fight that he was about to enter.

He knew that he lived to experience the good fight and he knew that he would love this exciting new challenge.

CHAPTER EIGHTEEN

Adam quickly looked around to get a feel for the ebb and flow of the ongoing battle.

He notched an arrow and sent it through an enemy warrior's skull.

In the background, he could hear the firing of automatic weapons as his crew members got themselves into the fight.

In the light of the blazing grass huts, Adam could see many of the friendly tribe people on the ground, but there were many more of them on their feet fighting together with his crew against their mortal enemy.

The invading humans were beginning to fall back, throwing their torches at the crew members and the friendly natives.

Sheer maddened anger and the lust for battle drove Adam forward.

He raced after several of the retreating enemy, bellowing mindlessly as he fired his remaining arrows into them and then took a spear from a fallen warrior and charged at the enemy with all the fury that had been pent up inside him just waiting for this release.

He easily knocked down the first of the enemy to take a stand before him with a side-long swipe of the spear.

Another enemy loomed at his side, and he drove the spear point into this stomach.

He screamed as he yanked the spear free, and slashed it across the face of another one.

It seemed to be a lot longer, but within seconds, his spear was bloodied along its entire length, slippery in his grasp as he slaughtered anyone who came within his reach.

Most of the remaining enemy warriors bolted, wide-eyed with new found fear as he raced after them, killing, killing again and again as he caught up with the slower moving enemy.

Behind him he could hear the shouts of the crew members and others growing fainter.

He followed the retreating warriors toward the distant cave-dotted cliffs.

One of them stumbled and fell in front of him. Adam drove his spear through him and felt it bite into his enemy's body.

The invaders were scattering in all directions, their weapons thrown away as they ran for their lives to escape his bloody rage.

He slowed down and turned to look back. He saw that Wyat, Eve and all the others were waving both arms over their heads triumphantly and yelling out at him to come back to where they were.

Adam ignored all of the distractions and pressed onward toward those caves in the distance where he knew the invaders had come from.

When he finally got there, it was still dark by the base of the cliff. Not even the glow from the burning village of his friends cast much light there.

But in that hushed gloom, where even the insects and beasts of the night lay silenced and frightened by the rush of fighting men, he heard breathing and the soft tread of bare feet on the stone ground.

He moved forward into the caves as if he were unaware of their presence.

But the instant they leaped at him, he whirled around and swung his spear at their legs like a scythe, cutting the three of them down.

As they fell in a jumbled heap, he hefted the bloody spear in his right hand and threw it at the nearer of the enemy who were trying to circle behind him.

The solid "THUNK" of the spear hitting his chest was louder than the desperate little gasp he gave out as he died.

Adam was able to kill the second warrior with a quick throw of his knife, but the third and last enemy, was already running down the darkening tunnel.

The deeper cave that Adam was now entering was absolutely pitch black inside, with not a single glowing ember from outside to light up its yawning blackness.

Dark as it was, Adam plunged into it anyway, still hot with his reckless fury.

It was the cave bear's warning growl that saved his life.

If the beast had been as intent on killing as Adam was, it would have waited quietly until Adam had blundered into its grasp, and then crushed him with its mighty paws.

But it was only an animal defending its lair, and it had none of the malicious hatred that human beings carry with them.

The cave bear was a massive animal that lived in Europe and parts of Asia, and they often sought shelter within deep caves that were dotted throughout the area.

The males often got as large as nine hundred pounds which is about three times the size of the brown bears of the future years.

Adam had heard about this type of cave bear. They grew extremely large along with the wooly mammoth, wooly rhinoceros' and cave lions.

The animal that he was facing growled once before it slashed out at him with a deadly paw.

Adam lunged forward at the sounds that the huge animal was making with all three of the spears that he had bundled together in his firm grasp.

Adam was very lucky.

He hit the bear's heart or lungs with the wild thrust.

One of the spears snapped in his hands, but the other two penetrated and the animal died with a hideous shriek of anger and agony.

Suddenly the blood lust cooled completely from Adam.

He was dripping with sweat, covered with blood from head to toe, trembling with physical exertion and emotional exhaustion.

Killing other men meant very little to Adam.

But the killing of this innocent animal snapped him out of his battle fury.

There, in the utter darkness of the beast's cave, he bent over and fell to his knees, panting and weeping with shame and regret over what he had just done.

TO BE CONTINUED

WHO IS THE REAL BUD SELIGSON, AUTHOR?

BUD SELIGSON, who was born in Chicago, Illinois, has been a "ghost writer" to many of the major, well-known writers of today's fiction and science fiction. He is also well known in Hollywood as a "story doctor" to several studios. Bud lives in Los Angeles with his wife Diane, who is his co-writer and sometimes editor.